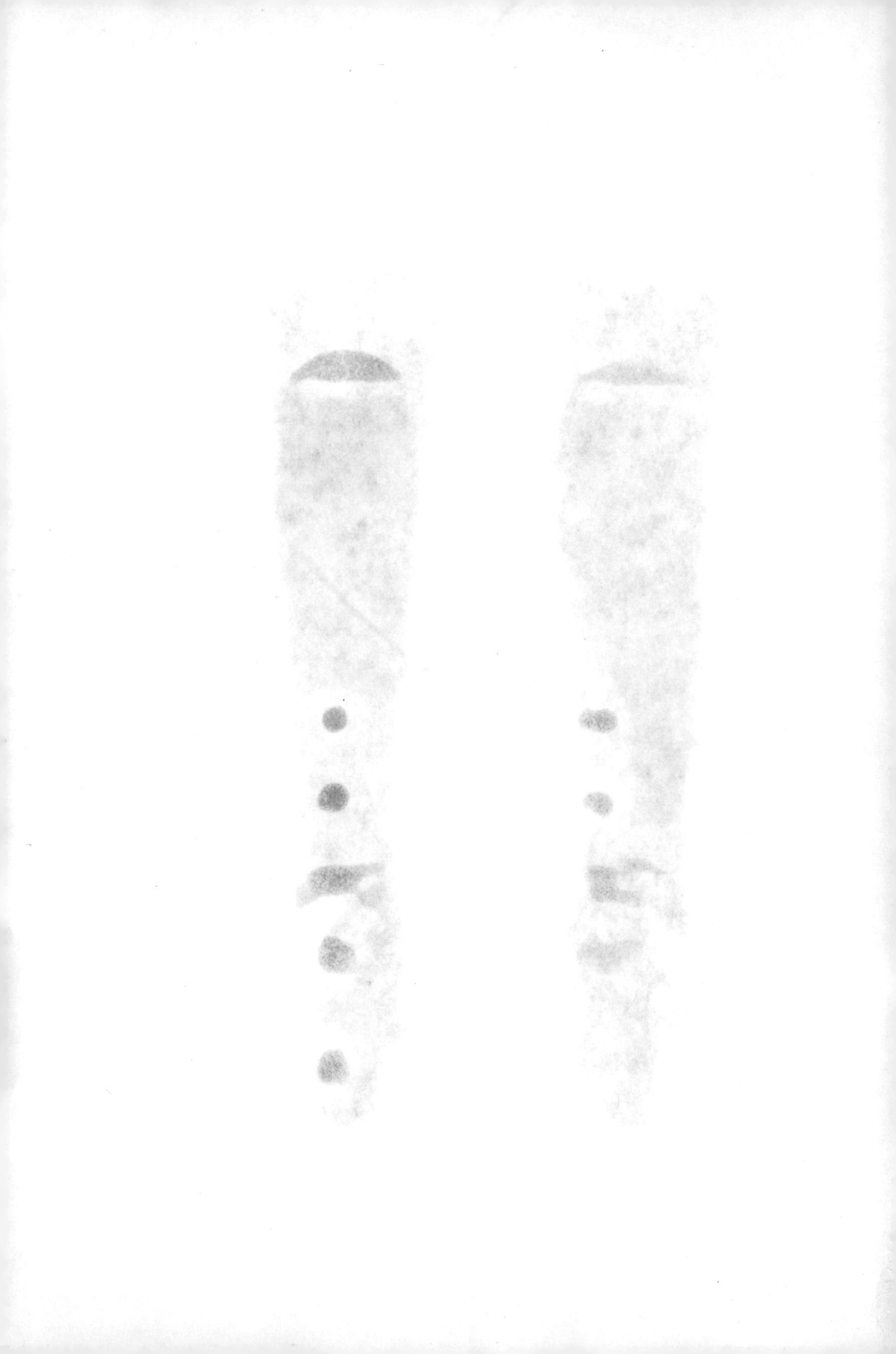

THE VISITING PHYSICIAN

Susan Richards Shreve

THE VISITING PHYSICIAN

Published in Large Print by arrangement with Doubleday,
an imprint of Bantam Doubleday Dell Publishing Group, Inc.
in the United States and Canada.

Wheeler Large Print Book Series.

Set in 16 pt. Plantin.

Library of Congress Cataloging-in-Publication Data

Shreve, Susan Richards.
The visiting physician / Susan Richards Shreve.
p. cm.—(Wheeler large print book series)
ISBN 1-56895-369-0 (lg. print)
1. City and town life—Ohio—Fiction. 2. Women physicians—Fiction. 3. Sick children—Fiction. 4. Missing children—Fiction. 5. Documentary films—Production and direction—Fiction. 6. Ohio—Fiction. 7. Large type books. I. Title. II. Series.
[PS3569.H74V57 1996b]
813'.54—dc20 96-34280
CIP

To Gilbert and Elisabeth and Matthew
with love

The Visiting Physician

I.
The Way Things Are
1. 3
2. 11

II.
Water Damage
The Story of Meridian: Monday, April 9
3. 32
4. 41
5. 53
6. 63

III.
Heart Scan
The Story of Meridian: Tuesday, April 10
7. 84
8. 91
9. 109
10. 119

IV.
Weather Report
The Story of Meridian:
Wednesday, April 11
11. 152

12. 168
13. 176
14. 183

V.
Visual Memory
The Story of Meridian:
Thursday, April 12
15. 208
16. 224

VI.
Do No Harm
The Story of Meridian: Friday, April 13
17. 262
18. 272
19. 277
20. 286

I.
The Way Things Are

1.

The afternoon sun spread a golden ribbon across the railroad tracks, coloring the faces lining the station platform a deep-crusted yellow. WELCOME TO MERIDIAN, the sign over the stationmaster's door said. Beside it, half obscured by a new poster of a missing child and written in red, were the words "the pure products of America" used to advertise the three-part television series on the town of Meridian broadcast by CBS in early May.

The missing child was a dark-haired angel described as: "Maggie Sailor, age 4, black hair, blue eyes, weight 30 pounds, reported missing May 10. Last seen at Bailey's pharmacy wearing a yellow Big Bird jacket and high tops. There is a strawberry birthmark on her left hip."

Someone, her mother perhaps, according to the stationmaster, had written in pen another "blue" so the information read "blue blue eyes" and had added "curly" with an asterisk before black hair. Someone else had made a Magic Marker mustache and dotted the child's cheeks with red spots. ZITS was written across her small and perfect nose.

"She's late," Reverend Benjamin Winters said, his arms folded tight across his narrow chest. He was a tall, awkwardly put-together man of unexpected temper, older than his pretty wife, whose choice of a profession in the service of God had come not of conviction but of deep misgivings. "What good is a doctor without a sense of time?" he asked of no one in particular.

"She's not late, Benjamin," Edith said, holding their baby daughter, taking the child with her everywhere since Maggie disappeared and now the terrible virus attacking the children of Meridian. "The train is late."

T. J. Wisely had brought the CBS film crew to Meridian in the first place. He sat now in a motorized wheelchair just at the end of the platform, his thick dark hair over the collar of his leather jacket, an eye patch over his left eye giving his strong, handsome face an aspect of practiced menace. Two years earlier, when a television director for whom T. J. was working had been looking for a small-town, preferably Midwestern—"a pure product of America is what I need," he said—T. J. had told him about Meridian.

The platform was crowded; about twenty people were there on the soft afternoon in late May waiting for the train from Detroit. Madeleine and Henry Sailor, the parents of the missing child, young parents, in their teens when Maggie was born, stood at the end of the platform beyond the crowd—stood straight and very close to one another, almost silent, although once Madeleine said, "I hope she is what we need," without looking at Henry, and Henry replied, folding his arms across his chest, "What we need in Meridian is a miracle."

Madeleine brushed imaginary lint from the front of her light cotton dress, a dress she had chosen for the occasion from the few selections in her closet, wishing to appear attractive and solid in spite of her shattered heart.

Henry was wearing the khaki trousers and plaid shirt he had on the day Maggie disappeared. He allowed Madeleine to wash them but otherwise he wore them every day, as if by his dress on the day of her disappearance he could recapture her life.

David Jaspersen, the young chief of police, stood near the Sailors with Winslow—his son Win, his only relation.

He was a large handsome man with extraordinary hands—thick and broad, with short fingers, hands that called attention to themselves; he had been a football player for Meridian and later tight end at the University of Wisconsin. Then he had gone to law school and married and had a son. In Meridian, he was considered a young man with an important future. No one expected him to return to a place of such diminished opportunities. But something happened to him in Wisconsin. He had never said. The year he was thirty-two he returned home with his baby son and trained as a policeman.

As chief of police, he held himself accountable

for the silent unraveling of trust since Maggie Sailor disappeared. The generous spirit of good will which had distinguished the town of his birth slipped away daily and he found himself able only to bear witness to what felt very much like the opening of a fault line in the tectonic plates beneath the earth on which Meridian sat.

"I'm surprised you're here to meet the doctor," David said to the Sailors.

"Reverend Winters asked us to come. He asked the congregation at church on Sunday to make her feel welcome," Henry Sailor said. "We didn't want to disappoint him."

"I hear she's very young," Madeleine Sailor said.

"She's young, but good, particularly with childhood diseases," David said. "I read the material sent on her from the hospital in Ann Arbor."

"Does she know she's walking into a nightmare?" Madeleine Sailor asked. "Does she know about Maggie?"

"She knows about the virus. Her specialty is pediatric immunology," David Jaspersen said. "She probably also knows about Maggie. Our bad news has been in the papers as far away as Washington, D.C."

"How come?" Win asked, pulling the brim of his baseball cap over his eyes.

"Since the film, people are interested in us—

even our misfortunes," David said. "In the last two weeks, the town is full of tourists."

Since the film aired on the first three days of May, tour buses and bicyclists on day trips and cars full of visitors on their way to Chicago or Cleveland stopped at Meridian to take a look at the town made suddenly famous by "The Story of Meridian" on CBS. It was on such a day, full of tourists taking pictures of Main Street, that Maggie had disappeared.

"The trouble with television is that people believe what they see on the screen and not their own lives," Henry Sailor said. "'The Story of Meridian' wasn't about us."

"I liked it better before we were on television." Win leaned against his father. "Except the parts when they filmed me playing Little League. That was good."

Meridian had been advertising for a physician since April, when Dr. Hazelton had suddenly gone to Michigan on a family emergency and then written that he would be taking an indefinite leave of absence.

For almost a month they had searched with no success. The letters came back from senior doctors that the town was too small, too isolated, that they should use the hospital in Harrisville, twenty-five miles south, that young doctors no longer wished to work without a partner, especially with the rise in malpractice suits.

But the truth was that the news about Meridian's troubles had appeared in stories released by the AP wires all over the Middle West. First there was Maggie Sailor's disappearance and then the floods, bringing a virus which could cause a perfectly healthy child to die. No young physician was willing to take on the responsibility alone for a small, isolated town suddenly at risk.

And then in May a call came from Dr. Helen Fielding, a pediatric resident at the University of Michigan, Ann Arbor, saying she was willing to come as a visiting physician until the crisis passed.

Meridian, Ohio, was settled in the early nineteenth century by the Welsh, chosen by them for its hills, like the hills of North Wales, with small valleys, always on the rise or on the fall, so a man standing was at an angle, coming up or going down. It was sheep land and, though the winter came in early and lasted, the summers were spectacular, with dazzling mornings and bright warm long afternoons.

A river ran through the center of town, which was why so small a place had a railway station, where freight trains were loaded with lumber that had been cut up north and floated downstream. The town itself was like a northern Italian town, with a narrow winding Main Street, and houses stacked like building blocks up the hill, rising above the village. The white-steepled Methodist church where Benjamin Winters was the minister was at one end of the main street and a small brick Roman Catholic church where Father

Thomas was the priest was at the other, so there was a kind of picture-book symmetry to the place, a quiet simple beauty with the frame houses painted white and lavender and yellow to cheer the spirit during the dark winter. To the hundreds of visitors who had come since the film to see the real Meridian, the town seemed to have fallen asleep. There were no chain stores; the television reception was poor, with only two channels, and cable had not come beyond Harrisville. The shops, even the grocery, were owned by local merchants. There was a small college founded by the Methodists which had been the first college in America to open its doors to women and to blacks, there were two elementary schools and a Catholic grammar school built to educate the Irish population who arrived in the Middle West after the potato famine in Ireland. There were two lawyers, Rubin and Rubin, brothers whose family had been among members of a failed Utopian community of Russian Jews near Philadelphia who had moved west with the railroad. Another descendant of that community owned the dry goods store and another the dry cleaners. There had been a colored section with families who came up from the South on the underground railroad in the nineteenth century before the Civil War and settled just beyond the train tracks. But after the flood of 1917 that section was washed out and everybody in Meridian lived in the houses built on the hills, lived together with a surprising spirit of well-wishing which was the quality the producers of "Meridian" had wanted to capture in the film.

The people of Meridian believed the river was responsible for their spirit of community. It was a long narrow river, almost a stream in the late summer and fall, called the river Meryn for the daughter of one of the Welsh settlers who drowned in it. In the spring, when the snows off the hills melted and spilled into the river, the ribbon of water flooded the banks of the Meryn, sometimes rising above the side roads, over the steps of houses, filling the basements, sometimes surging through Main Street like an army on the march, taking everything loose on the porches, in the yards, in front of shops, sometimes rising over the furniture, rotting the legs of tables, the must settling in for weeks.

The flooding came regularly in early May. Sometimes it was days of rain, then a small rush of river water over the banks; but there were years when the people of Meridian had to depend on one another like family. There was no predicting year to year how the river would go, so people lived prepared, with a sense of adventure and the kind of trust that comes of necessity.

In the distance, the long sad wail of the twelve-eleven from Detroit, running fifty minutes late, sounded and people along the platform straightened their shoulders, rearranged their clothes.

"Here it comes." David Jaspersen put his hands in his pockets.

"I see the light," Win said.

And the engine of the locomotive appeared curling around the corner, bearing down on the group gathered at the station with terrible speed.

A hundred yards away, the train slowed, crept the last distance, and stopped just at the point where David stood with his son. A conductor opened the door of the first coach, waved at the stationmaster, and lifted a suitcase down.

At the top of the steps a woman, much younger than the people of Meridian could possibly have imagined, with dark brown hair piled loosely on top of her head and an oval olive-skinned face out of another century, looked down at the waiting crowd.

"Hello," she said, not focusing on any one face in particular. She stepped down to the platform. "I believe someone is expecting a visiting physician."

2.

Helen Fielding saw the announcement for a physician on the bulletin board outside of the cafeteria of the university hospital in Ann Arbor in mid-April.

Small town in northwestern Ohio in search of a physician as temporary replacement in the practice of general medicine. Physician will be in charge of clinic with assistance from an excellent nurse. Housing provided. Charming yellow clapboard Victorian with three bedrooms and a garden. Contact Director, Medical School, University of Michigan.

Helen was not in search of a position. In fact just that morning before they got out of bed, Dr. Oliver Hampton had asked her to marry him. She didn't particularly want to marry Oliver, but she daydreamed of her own children. She had spent the morning in the pediatric clinic with telescopic scenes of domesticity interrupting her concentration. This is my daughter Christina, she said to herself as she examined the throat of a young patient, Christina, and my other children are at home, she went on in her mind's story, the fantasy reassuring, the children at home in permanent safety, Oliver at work, Helen capable of doctoring her own daughter, this Christina with a terrible strep throat. Which was how her thoughts were going at lunch break. She washed up, took two Bufferin for a persistent headache, changed to another white jacket and glanced at the bulletin board again. Something about the announcement captured her imagination.

"I believe it's the yellow Victorian house," she said to Oliver at lunch.

"You certainly can't be serious, Helen," he said.

She shrugged.

"I suppose you heard me this morning," he said.

"Of course." She lowered her voice so the other residents at the long Formica table would not overhear them. "It was just the house, Ollie," she said. "You know how I am about houses."

Underneath Helen's bed in the fourth-story apartment near the medical school were the boxes of pictures of houses which she had cut out since she arrived at Michigan from Mackinaw, where she had lived with her mother in a rooming house to which they had moved the year her father left, the year after Emma had died.

At night, before she went to bed, she leafed through issues of *Country Living* and *Home* and *House and Garden* for pictures of houses—whitewashed bedrooms with quilts on the canopy beds and fireplaces, kitchens with round tables, bowls of red apples glistening in the sun, living rooms with couches full of pillows, a table of books with candles, a vase of yellow wildflowers.

The people who knew Helen, who thought they knew her, her fellow students and other physicians at the hospital, found her enchanting, like a child without affectations. There was something unexpected, full of whimsy and unspoken promise: the way she wore her hair in a clumsy halo on top of her head, the way she dressed in long colorful skirts and blouses open at the neck.

She had a soft assured voice, a physical ease with people, a generosity of spirit. Not the demeanor of a woman of science.

There was a mystery about her, as if secrets, hormonal in the blood, altered the chemistry of her body, creating a kind of magnet for the imaginings of other people; she was the subject of small observations which accumulated, giving her a force.

Very little was actually known about Helen Fielding's life. She was the only remaining child of a professor of European history in Santa Cruz, California, and a mother who had, in the year Helen went off to college, gone to New York City with a younger man she'd met who was vacationing on Mackinaw Island where she lived. No one in medical school had met Helen's mother, who did not travel except the one trip to New York City. But her father, a man of charismatic warmth similar to Helen's, came once a year and stayed with Helen in her apartment for a week or so during which they would give cheerful dinners for other physicians, ordering in Chinese food.

She seldom lived alone in the small apartment on the fourth floor of Logan which she shared now with Oliver Hampton but before that for two years with Stephen Bryant and before that at the end of undergraduate school with Peter Tatler. Each man had felt as Oliver did that eventually he would marry Helen. She seemed exactly the kind of woman with whom to make a life. But at a moment of decision she'd slip away.

Oliver was astonished when Helen told him that she wouldn't marry him.

"Not ever?" he asked.

"Not now," she replied.

"But maybe later?" he asked.

"I don't know, Ollie," she said sadly. "There's something that keeps me from making a life."

She knew about falling in love and it worried her, left her in despair; she seemed unable to go beyond the high-spirited drunkenness of early romance. She had fallen in love with Oliver and Peter and Stephen and others but always briefly, a small conflagration that lit up her room and was gone.

Something was absent, as if a painting of Helen Fielding would show a young willowy woman, a stranger, not a face she recognized. Sometimes she'd clean her small apartment, bringing in forsythia, a brightly colored rug and, standing in the entrance, she'd survey the rooms, the living room with its black flowered chintz couch, the white bedroom with yellow freesias in a glass beside the bed, the study with her grandmother's small cherry desk. "This is where Helen Fielding lives," she'd say to herself. "The physician from Mackinaw Island. Do you know her?"

The only time she felt the passion she remembered from a childhood of strong feelings was when she cut out pictures of the warm crowded rooms in houses. Then she'd have a sudden rush of memory as if she could feel the physical warmth of the soft white comforter in the pictures of *House and Garden*. What she usually felt even in love affairs was an intellectual understanding of emotion, or the physical expressions of a rapid heartbeat, a general anxiety from too much carbon dioxide going out of the lungs, a dry mouth. But she didn't feel the emotion itself.

In May there was another notice on the bulletin board.

> *MERIDIAN. Small town in northwest Ohio in urgent need of a temporary physician. Floods and unusual heat have brought outbreak of a serious virus affecting small children. Contact David Jaspersen, 216*-843-2121, Meridian, Ohio 46537.

Helen sat at a table in the hospital cafeteria, a general sense of weakness overtaking her.

She knew Meridian, Ohio.

She knew Meridian very well, even the wet smell of it in summer, the sound of high wind in the voluminous trees, of the trains from Chicago, the mossy brick sidewalks—she knew the town with the fresh painting of a child's memory, although she hadn't been there since the hot, hot summer when she was four and Emma had been two.

She had a sudden picture of sunflowers against

white clapboard and the smell of sugar cookies baking. Until Emma died, her family had spent summers with her father's family in Meridian, her Great-Aunt Martha and Uncle Peter.

Dear Father [Helen wrote on a postcard to her father in Santa Cruz]. I'm moving to Meridian as a visiting M.D. for several months. They have a viral outbreak. It will be so odd to be back there. Will let you know my address, Love, H. P.S. Did you see the TV special, "The Story of Meridian"? They tell me there was a three-part series in early May but I was on rotation and didn't hear about it.

Dear Mother [she wrote to her mother]. I will be moving shortly to Meridian as a visiting physician. They have suffered the loss of children recently—so far one little girl has died from a terrible virus brought on by floods—and one has disappeared. So they are desperate for a doctor. Unfortunately, I am going alone as Oliver Hampton—remember Ollie from your wedding, the one with the wire-rimmed glasses and British?—has met someone else. Love, Helen. P.S. When we visited, you never told me that the river is called Meryn for a little girl who drowned in it.

She thought to cross out the P.S. before she folded the letter and put it in the envelope but did not. Writing to her mother and father made her so anxious that she stopped at the pharmacy after she mailed the letters and bought a pack of cigarettes, smoking several, one after the other, while she stood on the corner leaning against a stop sign, then she threw the pack away.

On the train to Cleveland, Helen had trouble breathing. It was not unfamiliar. She had had trouble breathing before. She sat very still, her hands folded in her lap, her eyes closed. In her role as her own mother, she whispered to herself: "You're fine, Helen darling—it's a big step to return to the place you went as a child, where Emma disappeared—but you'll be absolutely fine, I promise." She held her own hand.

"Are you all right?" the young woman in the seat across from Helen asked.

"Fine," Helen said quickly, her eyes flying open. "I'm perfectly fine," she said without thinking. She reached in her book bag and got out a package of peanut M and M's, peanut butter crackers and two Bufferin.

"Would you like some?" she asked, opening the M and M's, offering them to the young woman.

"Thank you," the woman said. "I love anything chocolate."

And gradually they fell to talking about medicine and the young woman's children, and houses in which the woman also had an interest, having recently bought a new one. Helen was pleased with the ease of conversation, which had the feel of friendship, reassured that she could make a friendship out of nothing, even with a stranger.

When the woman got off the train—they had not exchanged addresses, only names: Lynn Sorrell was the one belonging to the stranger—Helen felt an unexpected loss.

In the small foul-smelling toilet of the train south, she examined her face up close in the mirror, her dark blue eyes flecked with yellow, familiar eyes, but more pained than she imagined them when she thought of the face that others saw, a warm comforting face, as she imagined it, with an expression of an inner peace of mind.

The young woman on the train had seen the film about Meridian and read the stories about the killer virus in a Pittsburgh paper. Two days ago she had even seen a picture of the missing child flash on the television screen after the local news.

"I watch a lot of TV," she said. "You're braver than I would be. I couldn't be in a town where something is happening to the children."

Helen looked in the full-length mirror on the back of the door to the toilet, pleased with what the people of Meridian would be seeing soon. She was tall with long legs and full breasts which she emphasized in her way of dressing in V-necked shirts and blouses like the one she had on now. The impression was of a woman too fulsome to be a model but beautiful with a kind of soft maternal beauty.

⋆ ⋆ ⋆

The train traveled through hilly farmland, lambing country, bright in the afternoon sun. Helen opened her backpack which held mostly books: the May *Country Living* and *House Beautiful,* a medical dictionary, a Random House paperback dictionary, *Anna Karenina,* which she always carried, preferring to read a familiar story rather than to start a new one. She took out the dictionary and opened to the word "meridian." She liked definition 3 particularly: "the great circle of the celestial sphere that passes through its poles and the observer's zenith." She looked up "zenith."

One of the important things she had learned as a student of medicine had to do with fate. She was not by nature accommodating to the forces of fate; rather more likely to believe in the power of her own will. But science required certain personal adjustments. What Helen Fielding was doing on this train headed south toward Meridian, Ohio, felt to her very much like destiny.

II.
Water Damage

The Story of

Merdian

Monday, April 9

The film crews had arrived in early April and set up shop in the First Methodist Church. They chose it because of the large assembly room in the parish hall next door, and the Sunday school rooms were turned into bedrooms for the crew. The director, a taciturn young man called Peter Forester whose temperament showed no evidence of a childhood in a benevolent small town, liked the church because it had the look of picture postcards, white with a steeple and a simple cross, built at the highest point of Main Street so the cross seemed to float disembodied above the town. A clock was on the tower of the church, stopped, since anyone could remember, at three-fifteen, although Benjamin Winters had tried to get it fixed when Meridian painted all of the buildings on Main Street including First Methodist for the arrival of the crew.

"It's nice the way the clock has stopped at three-fifteen," Peter Forester said to T. J. with the breezy arrogance of a man accustomed to the last word. "It's a metaphor, you know. After all, the film is about stopped clocks."

"I don't like this," Edith Winters said the first night after CBS crews arrived, lying in bed next to Benjamin, keeping her daughter at her breast long after the child had stopped sucking. "It feels dangerous."

"Dangerous?" Benjamin was pleased to have the film crew, pleased with the importance suddenly attending his ministry which, except during the season of floods, was a long repetition of changeless days.

"It's dangerous to have a lot of strangers sleeping in the church at night, making up stories about us." She slid under the covers, turning her back to her husband. "Don't kiss me," she said when he leaned over her.

"The story *is* true," Benjamin said. "We're a small town with an unusual sense of community."

"We were ordinary until they told us we weren't," Edith said. "I feel looked at."

"By people sleeping in the next building? What's the matter with you, Edith?"

"By people who've come pretending to know us," she said crossly.

"Think of it as moral," Benjamin said while she put the baby to bed in the bassinet in their room.

"I don't think of anything as moral," Edith said.

"T. J. tells me the point of his film is moral," Benjamin said. "That people in America have lost their sense of good will toward one another." Benjamin sat up in bed, putting his pillow behind him. "He says the documentary is a call to action, reminding people of the way we used to be."

Edith crossed her arms and sat down in the rocking chair.

"I'm sleeping here tonight in case of a fire," she said.

"A fire?"

"In case they set the church on fire." She pulled her legs up and rested her chin on her knees.

"Suit yourself, Edie," Benjamin said, turning away from the light, staring at the shadows playing across the white walls of the bedroom, waiting for a hint of sleep although there did not seem a chance for sleeping with the rocking of Edith's chair against the hardwood floor.

"Benjamin?" she said after a while. "Are you awake?"

"Quite awake," he said.

"This just feels wrong to me," she said. "I can't explain it."

Days like these with the smell of spring in the air, David Jaspersen ached for a woman. Not a woman he'd go after but one who would take after him, lay her hand on the back of his neck—"I've been thinking about you, David," she'd say—and the touch of her hand was silk.

During nights of this unbearable aching he'd wander the house restless, imagining a woman in his room, imagining the smell of her, her back curved graceful as a willow leaning down to undress.

On the first night the film crew arrived in Meridian, he found himself imagining women again.

He had exhausted Meridian easily when he returned home with Win in September of his thirty-second year. There were the girls he'd known in high school—married now but young enough for a sprinkle of interest. There was Mary Rubin just out of college, too young for him but pretty and very smart. And there was Sophie. Sophi-a, she called herself. He liked to think of her stretched out on his soft white sheets sleeping, her thick dark hair against the white pillow.

But he had no future with Sophie—she was a child herself, with a child's offhand innocence and the quality of a stray, a wanderer in the backyards of other people's lives. Besides, she had Molly. There was no telling how she and Molly got by day to day, neighbors, probably. Something was askew about her, something wild rattling in her brain, and David knew he ought to steer clear although he had a yearning to save her.

Nevertheless she was recklessly on his mind when T. J. Wisely knocked at the door, wheeled into the living room and dragged himself onto the couch, lifting his legs beside him.

"Jeez," T. J. said. "I killed my back playing basketball with the crew. Do you have a beer?"

"This is my last one," David said.

"What about a whisky?"

David poured Scotch into a glass and sat down across from T. J.

"Maybe you should give up basketball now you're in a wheelchair," he said. "Set some limits on your life."

"I'm good at it," T. J. said. "I'm still very good even on wheels. You ought to come out and play with us. There's a guy on the camera crew who used to play for N. C. State."

"I'm not that good, although I could probably outrun you." David put his feet up on the coffee table. "I suppose you've come over to talk about the film."

"Nope. All that's A-OK. The crew's settled in the good reverend's church. The reverend is pleased to have some action in the house of God and they're all set on the shoots for tomorrow." He turned over on his side facing David, his arm resting on his hand. "I've come about Sophie," he said.

"Sophie? I didn't know Sophie was in your busy life."

T. J. pulled a cigarette out of his pocket. "In a way, she is," he said.

"Well, you should get her out, T. J.," David said. "You've had a hard enough time as it is without asking for trouble."

T. J. Wisely had arrived alone by train in

Meridian when he was three years old, according to the doctor who had examined him shortly after his arrival. The conductor of the train from Chicago had told the stationmaster in Meridian that T. J. had been put on the train in Chicago by a young woman of forgettable description who said his name was T. J. Wisely and he was to get off at Meridian where he would be met by his Uncle Bob. "We have a lot of Bobs here," the stationmaster said but not one of them was there to pick up T. J. when he arrived so he stayed with David Jaspersen's family while the police searched in Chicago for the woman. And later he became a ward of Meridian, a mascot, everybody's child. He was adaptable, assuming the demeanor of the family with whom he happened to be living at the time, the manner of dress, the pattern of speech, the daily mass or weekly church suppers, the standards for studying and behavior, the grades expected. Chameleon-like, he slipped through childhood beloved and then to everyone's surprise, because T. J. had shown no great love of danger, he left just after his eighteenth birthday and went to Los Angeles to become a stunt man in the movies.

"What would you expect from a boy whose mama puts him on a train to nowhere?" David Jaspersen's mother said to him the year T. J. left.

"So tell me about Sophie," David said.

"We've got to do something about her before this film gets going. She doesn't fit the picture."

"I don't get what you mean," David said. "She's a sweet troubled woman."

"Sweet maybe and certainly troubled," T. J. said. "But here we have this story of America like it used to be, pure as the driven snow. That's the idea, right?"

"It's your film," David said.

"So on walks Sophie DeLaurentis with her pouty lips, Eve in the garden of Eden." He rolled his eyes. "I don't think so."

"So cut her out of it after the filming is done," David said. "Most of a film ends up on the cutting-room floor, isn't that right?"

"Usually," T. J. said. "But unfortunately the director of this particular film met her at dinner tonight and WHAMMO. 'She's perfect,' Peter Forester said to me. 'She's a born-again Marilyn with black hair.' "

David shrugged. "You're the film guys," he said. "The rest of us are simply products of your imagination."

Sophie DeLaurentis was still awake when David called.

"Do you have something going with T. J.?" he asked.

"T. J.?" she asked. "What makes you think that, David?"

"Call it a leap of faith," David said.

"Uh-uh," she said, yawning a long-drawn-out yawn. "I don't have anything going on now with anyone but I met the director of the TV show tonight and he sort of liked me."

"So I understand."

"He said he hoped to get me in the show a lot," she said. "And Molly too. He thinks Molly is beautiful."

"Well, be careful," David said.

"Of what?" Sophie asked. "There's nothing to be afraid of."

"Just be careful."

Sophie didn't go back to bed after the chief of police called. She thought of him as the chief of police, liking that he was *somebody* in Meridian and she had seen him naked. Or he had seen her naked. She wasn't sure which she liked better since she knew David Jaspersen no better without his clothes than she knew him in full uniform with his hat on. He was a covered-up man.

She took off her pale pink nightgown with the lacy bib, checking Molly to see if she was sleeping soundly since she didn't want her little daughter to see her looking at her own naked body in the full-length mirror on the closet door.

She had a soft fleshy body with a little round pocket of a belly and downy cushions on her high hips, full wavy hair other women would die for, and large blue eyes. "Wonder eyes," Dr. Hazelton had said to her when he first came back to Meridian from medical school and wanted Sophie to reciprocate his urgent love, which she refused. But she slept with him. That Sophie would do with almost anyone. She picked up the telephone and called him now, keeping her voice soft not to wake Molly.

"Hello, Rich," she said.

"I'm glad you called," Richard Hazelton said coolly. "I saw you at the coffee shop today with the film crew and I wanted to talk to you about that."

"The director wants to make me sort of a star," Sophie said. "That's why I called to tell you that I can't bring Molly to her appointment tomorrow."

"I don't want Molly in this movie," Richard Hazelton said.

"It's not a movie."

"I don't want her in whatever it is," he said crossly.

"She's my child," she said. "It's my choice."

"Not just your child, Sophie."

"I say she is," Sophie said.

"We'll see," Dr. Hazelton said, hanging up. He always was the one to hang up first.

T. J. opened the front door of the parish hall and went in. Most of the crew had already gone to bed, the doors to the Sunday school pulled shut, but at the back there was a small party with Peter Forester and Marina, his assistant, and Pleeper Jones, the new production assistant, sitting in metal chairs with their feet up drinking beers. T. J. took a beer out of the fridge.

"I'm going to like doing this film," Peter said, lifting his glass to T. J. in the gesture of a toast.

"Meridian is a lot more interesting a town than I had thought when we came to scout it in the fall."

T. J. pulled a chair up beside Marina.

"What interests you besides Sophie DeLaurentis?" T. J. asked.

Peter rolled his eyes. "I can see creating a real masterpiece in 'Meridian' if we choose the shoots carefully and do some amazing camera work," he said. "So brighten up, T. J. You're a genius to have brought us here."

3.

It was an odd little party that greeted Helen as she got off the train in Meridian. A group, in its earnest formality, out of a different time, more English than American, the way they lined up and shook the doctor's hand, a spirit of expectancy concealing their fragile lives.

Helen had anticipated the person named on the notice would meet her train, the man called David Jaspersen. She hadn't imagined him a policeman, certainly not chief of police, which was how he introduced himself, the first in an assembly line of greeters, then Reverend Benjamin Winters and Edith Winters with their daughter and a professor from the philosophy department at Meridian College, the stationmaster, a banjo player who ran the coffee shop and children from the grammar school, a reporter from the newspaper, the pharmacist, the man who owned the Exxon station and had been the only adult to contact the virus so far but was almost recovered, the widow of a soldier who had died in Vietnam, Madeleine and Henry Sailor.

"I'm the mother of Maggie," Mrs. Sailor said anxiously. "You may have seen her picture on television."

The man in the wheelchair was last but Helen had noticed him as soon as she got off the train. Noticed his extraordinary face, not entirely handsome but so dark and striking that the force of it struck her.

"I'm T. J. Wisely," he said with a small odd wave, but he seemed to be on a mission and wheeled past her, up the hill in front of the station, going quite fast.

"T. J. was one of the producers of the television series about us," David Jaspersen said, taking her duffel bag over his shoulder. "It aired three weeks ago."

"If you haven't seen it, we have a tape," Benjamin Winters said, taking Helen's medical bag and her small backpack.

Helen followed them across the street and down Main Street; even the smell was familiar, a river smell, dank, a little fishy, not entirely unpleasant. She wondered should she tell these new friends that Meridian was familiar to her, that her Aunt Martha lived in the white cottage above the Catholic church on Main Street. Perhaps when she was little Helen had even played with one of them—David Jaspersen didn't seem older than thirty, which was her age.

"I was surprised at the receiving line," she said to David, walking along beside him with Edith Winters, a pretty light-bodied woman, and her bright-eyed baby daughter.

"We wanted to make you feel welcome," Ben Winters said.

"You've made me feel very welcome," Helen said.

But the welcome was weighted with expectation.

"We've had a terrible Spring," David Jaspersen was saying.

"And a hard time persuading a physician to come here temporarily," Ben Winters said.

"We think the film might have discouraged doctors from coming," David said. "There was so much publicity."

"But the film was positive, wasn't it?" Helen asked.

"It's what has happened since the film crews left." David shifted Helen's duffel bag to the other shoulder. "One of our children is missing and now this virus."

Edith Winters stopped at the corner of Lace Street and Main. "She disappeared right here from the front of the drugstore on the tenth of May," Edith said. "Her mother was just in the store getting Advil for migraines and a hot water bottle because their second floor doesn't have heat." She took Helen by the wrist. "Did you see the poster about Maggie in the station?"

"I didn't, although I've heard about her," Helen said. "A woman I met on the train saw the notice of her disappearance on television."

"We've become celebrities," Edith Winters said.

"And now this virus," Helen said. "Tell me about it."

"The virus comes on suddenly," David Jaspersen said. "A child gets up in the morning with a slight fever. By noon she'll be burning with fever and panting for breath."

"Only one child has died," Edith Winters said. "Stephanie Burns died last week. But who knows? You'll see. Some of the children look terrible."

"We've thought of rats, although we haven't seen any in town," David said.

"Or bats," Benjamin Winters said. "I had a cousin die of a fungus from bat excrement and we do have bats."

"Stephanie's brother Kenny came down with it in the middle of last night," Ben Winters said. "Did you know that, David?"

"I did. I talked to Mrs. Burns this morning," he said. "We have a report of fourteen children ill as of yesterday afternoon," David said. "One was brought into the clinic this morning."

"Who?" Ben Winters asked.

"Beatrice Tallis," David said.

"Who's at the clinic with her?" Helen asked, following David Jaspersen up the hill toward the brightly colored houses along the second tier of houses beyond Main Street.

"A nurse," Edith said.

"Prudential's not exactly a nurse," David Jaspersen said.

"She's as good as a nurse," Edith said. She turned to Helen. "You'll see."

The sun climbed directly overhead, lighting the tops of houses, casting a spider web of shadows on the ground in front of where they were walking.

They passed the market and the dry goods store and the volunteer fire department, a cluster of small houses directly on the street whose front doors opened to the sidewalks as houses do in Eastern European villages.

Aunt Martha's was painted blue now with a peach-colored front door. A young woman with a small child was sweeping the front porch. The woman was tall and slender with soft brown wavy hair, and what Helen saw was her own mother sweeping the front porch while Aunt Martha, in the kitchen, sliced tomatoes for sandwiches and Emma, a powder puff of yellow curls, stood on a chair in the kitchen and crayoned orange and red kittens in her coloring book.

Days, months went by and she never thought of Emma at all; seldom was there even a picture of her sister in her mind—now this lump in her throat as if she were growing a tumor.

They stopped at the end of Main Street at a small Victorian house painted purple with a white front porch and trim, a cheerful, comical house, unlikely as a medical clinic.

"When the film crews were coming, we painted all of the houses along Main Street," Ben Winters said. "We were told that color is good on television so we went all out."

"The purple was Prudential's idea," David said. "She said it was the color of redemption."

"Resurrection," Ben Winters corrected.

"Whatever," David Jaspersen said.

He opened the front door, dropping Helen's bag on a chair. The reception room was empty. It was a large room with long windows and window seats covered in lavender, striped chairs, flowers on the desk, pale peach stock and daisies drooping with age, wicker couches and rocking chairs, baskets of toys lined up against the wall, a worn oriental rug, faded blue and beige. Someplace music was playing. David checked his watch.

"Where's Prudential?" Ben Winters asked.

"I wonder," David said.

"She said she'd be here to meet us when we came," Ben said.

"I know," David said. "I talked to her at ten."

Ben led the way through the reception room, opening the door to the examining rooms.

"You have only one nurse?" Helen asked.

David nodded.

"With a possible epidemic, I'll need more than one nurse," Helen said.

"Wait until you meet Prudential," David said.

Helen followed David and Benjamin Winters down the hall, past a room with a half-closed door, another room, whose door was open—the examining table in disarray, the odor of disinfectant fog-thick in the corridor.

A tiny lavender girl lay on the examining table, her face still damp with perspiration, her pale red hair matted to her face.

"I had a terrible feeling," Benjamin Winters said.

Helen's breath caught in her throat. She went over to where the child lay, hoping to give the impression of competence although she felt as if she couldn't breathe. She examined the little girl, checking her pulse, her ears, her locked mouth, lifting her eyelids, her eyes fixed in death.

She had never worked without a staff, without other doctors or professors of medicine or laboratory technicians. The absolute aloneness of her life in Meridian struck her suddenly with a sweep by doubt.

In her short life as a physician she had seen dead children—there was the child from Archman, Michigan, who died in a fall from a horse—Helen was on emergency room duty when they brought her in and was the only one with her when she died—the farm boy from meningitis and the enchanting Chinese boy from chicken pox and Patricia on the operating table for an appendectomy when Helen was on a surgery rotation. Their small faces, whole scenes of their swift departure, stayed with Helen, rolled through her mind, kept her awake at night—but she didn't feel implicated.

Her deep pleasure as a young pediatrician had to do with the lives she had saved, the children for whom her presence had made a difference. She was considered a gifted diagnostician. She had certainly been responsible for diagnosing Reye's syndrome in Mary Harter, just in time or she would have died, and an unusual stomach cancer in Tom Bruin which probably saved his life, and peritonitis when Rebecca Slade was being treated for constipation.

But here in the sunny room of the Meridian Clinic standing beside the body of a child, no one for miles around with medical authority except the chief of police, who ought at least to have an up-to-date certificate in Emergency Medical Training, but maybe not, Helen was worried.

Behind her there was a shuffle and when she turned around a woman was standing in the doorway, her long-fingered hand on her hip.

"If you're writing up a death certificate, the time was twelve forty-eight and I was with her when she died," she said. "Her mother is on sedatives I gave her."

Prudential—she had no last name that she gave out; too many husbands over the years, she said—was blue black, with skin that glistened waxy and a large head with a broad forehead. Not a trace of a smile.

"I'm Helen Fielding," Helen said, extending her hand.

"I know who you are," Prudential said, folding her arms across her chest, refusing Helen's extended hand. "I can't touch you. I've got death on my hands."

"So do I," Helen said, conscious of the woman's height, how much taller she was.

Prudential shrugged. "Now you're here, I'm leaving for about fifteen minutes to tend to something at home," she said. "Clinic hours don't start again until two-thirty."

"That's fine," Helen said. "I'll find my way around."

"I called the funeral parlor," Prudential said. "Mr. Rubin will be here shortly." Prudential walked with a limp but she walked fast and she was down the corridor and out the door before Helen had a chance to speak.

"I hope you won't be sorry you came here," David Jaspersen said, pulling shut the door where the child Beatrice lay.

"I won't be," Helen replied.

But following him back down the corridor to the waiting room, lightheaded, her palms cold and damp, she took small drinks of air to keep from fainting.

4.

David Jaspersen left after Prudential. He said he would be back later to show Helen the house where she'd be living and that Mr. Rubin, the undertaker, would be along to collect Beatrice Tallis.

"Can't you stay?" Helen wanted to ask but he had gone.

At the main desk she skimmed the medical files in a tray beside the telephone, hoping for a call to divert her from the child in the examining room behind her chair, any call requiring her attention.

In the office was a supply closet and she checked what was available—in fact very little for a town of any size—samples of penicillin and erythromycin which she hoped might be useful for this illness but there was only enough for a day or two of sick children. She would order a pathology report on Beatrice Tallis. She telephoned a distributor in Toledo for more erythromycin in case the illness was bacterial and could be treated by an antibiotic.

Then she put in a call to her pediatric professor

in Ann Arbor. The child in the examining room had almost certainly died of respiratory failure.

"Legionella," he agreed. A water-borne bacteria washed into Meridian with a flood in early May could have brought legionella. If the illness was caught in time before the patient's respiratory system shut down, erythromycin was successful.

She called her mother but the answering machine was on with her mother's soft melodic voice. "We hope you'll leave a message after the beep." The answering machine was always on when Helen called. Not that she never talked with her mother. Alice Fielding did call, not often, but she usually returned Helen's calls, sometimes hours later, sometimes days. Helen imagined her standing at her easel in the studio off the kitchen of her New York City apartment listening to Helen's voice—"Mama, just calling to see how you are, I'm here. Call me whenever." She ought to scream, "Mama—Mama, pick up the telephone. I see you there listening to me." But she never raised her voice with her mother, afraid that Allie Fielding might disappear altogether if Helen went after her like that.

"I'm in Meridian at the clinic," she said now. "I'll call you with my new number tonight. Hugs and kisses," she added. "Wherever you are."

Prudential's telephone number was taped to the desk and Helen dialed. It rang twice and the receiver seemed to shake off the cradle but no one spoke.

"Hello," Helen said. "Prudential?"

She waited for a reply.

"Is anybody there?"

There was a shuffle at the other end and then the receiver dropped.

When the telephone finally rang in the clinic, it was Reverend Winters saying he would be with Beatrice Tallis's family for the rest of the day. He gave Helen the telephone number, which she wrote down, wondering should she go to the Tallises' house, if that's what Ben Winters had wanted from her when he called, as if medicine in a small town required personal contact. She was more concerned by the anticipation of a relationship with the family of the dead child than with the death of the child itself, accustomed to medicine in a laboratory. She had seen parents, of course, standing in the corridor of the Ann Arbor hospital, outside their child's hospital room, and she of course had spoken to them about the condition of their child, but always protected by the limitations of a hospital setting. She was never expected at dinner or required to engage in prolonged conversation of a personal nature with the parents of a child who had died. When she thought of it now, imagining the range of responsibilities in a small town where she was the only doctor, it was as if the opening of this Pandora's box would bring a sufficient flood of tears to drown her.

Mr. Rubin the undertaker didn't come. She went to the window overlooking Main Street, with its line of shops, an ice cream store under a red-striped awning, a toy shop, a laundromat. She didn't remember these shops from her childhood—certainly not the ice cream store. Uncle Peter and Aunt Martha used to take her to a park with picnic tables and swings. Sometimes Emma went along. Not often because her mother didn't trust Aunt Martha. "Aunt Martha is awfully old to watch a two-year-old," her mother used to tell her. "Something might happen to Emma." She was not too old to swing Helen high over the bank or spread a picnic of fried chicken and biscuits on a bright tablecloth under the willow tree. But Helen didn't remember visits to an ice cream shop. Now she opened the front door, wishing there were someone in Meridian she knew, some friend, someone she could call.

Down Main Street to the left was a small white clapboard cottage next to a playground empty of children, a jungle gym, a basketball court. No doubt the parents of Meridian were afraid to send their children out to play. Beyond, the streets were empty. Next to the white clapboard cottage was a very slender building painted barn red with black shutters and a long yellow banner hanging out the second-story window with MAGGIE written across the length of it.

As Helen watched, the man called T. J. maneuvered his wheelchair out the front door with a pile of papers on his lap. She was glad to see him, glad for company, and waved a shy half wave.

"I heard," he said, wheeling across the street.

"About the child?" Helen asked.

He nodded.

"Beatrice Tallis."

"I know," he said. "It's an awful welcome to Meridian."

"It's why I came here." She sat down on the top step to be at his level. "What do you have there?" she asked.

He handed her one of the bright yellow fliers with a picture of a small dark-haired beauty—a tiny clear picture—and underneath in simple, bold print was written:

MAGGIE SAILOR IS GONE
Contact T. J. Wisely
MAGGIE Headquarters
216-431-0011

"David may have told you," he said. "I used to be in Hollywood until I had this accident."

"He didn't say."

"I was a stunt man and fell," he said. "For the last two weeks I've been looking for Maggie full time."

His voice seemed far away, across the street, in another room. She felt lightheaded.

"You know about Maggie?"

She nodded. "I do," she said.

"Keep some fliers," T. J. said. He touched her arm. "Are you okay? You look gray."

"I must be overtired," she said, handing the flier back to him, "but it's making me faint to look at the picture of her."

"I'm sorry," T. J. said. "You're probably exhausted."

"I can't stand missing children," Helen said.

Emma's body had not been found.

"It makes a difference to see a body," Helen's father had said years later, after the divorce. "To know."

"But you do know," Helen said.

"We assume," her father had said, but he wouldn't continue the conversation and her mother didn't speak of Emma at all.

What they did know was that, on a Saturday in late June, Helen and Emma had wandered away from the picnic tables in the park, across the field, to the woods along the river Meryn. Helen remembered standing on the bank, throwing pebbles into the river. She remembered Emma sitting on a large root, playing with a stick, her yellow curls wrapped in ribbons.

And then she was gone.

"Gone," Helen said to her mother, running back to the picnic grounds.

"Gone?" her mother said. "Just gone, like that? She can't be."

But she was.

"Try to remember, Helen," her mother said later as the fire department dragged the river, put out alerts in the adjoining towns. "First Emma was there sitting beside you and then she was gone?"

Helen nodded.

"What happened from the last moment you saw her to the moment you realized she was gone?" her father asked.

"I don't remember," Helen said. "I looked down and she was gone."

"T. J. is a peculiar man," Prudential said, her arms folded across her chest, watching Helen pack her medical bag with thermometers and alcohol and cotton and disposable hypodermics and bottles of erythromycin. "Not everybody's cup of tea."

"I like him," Helen said, and it was more than just an attraction, although certainly it was that. "I'm not sure why."

"If anybody can find Maggie Sailor, T. J. will be the one to do it." She shrugged. "It's in his blood."

Prudential checked through the files and pulled the ones for the children they would be visiting.

"So we're doing house calls. Dr. Hazelton never did house calls," Prudential said. "Even when Ben Winters's father had a heart attack,

Dr. Hazelton made him come into the office and he died here." She made the list: "Maria Walker, Laura O'Connor, Sallie Durham, Brian Bliss."

"Just four?"

"That'll take two hours," Prudential said.

Helen put a note on the front door that said WILL RETURN AT 5 P.M.

"I called you at home," she said to Prudential.

"I wasn't at home," she said.

She closed the door to the office and walked with Helen down the path to the street.

"Someone picked up the phone," Helen said casually, following Prudential away from the center of town.

"Someone did?"

"Maybe a child?" Helen said. "The receiver fell and then the line stayed open."

"I don't have a child," Prudential said. "I'm sixty-five years old."

They went first to Maria Walker's house, a small yellow house next to the Roman Catholic church with a gym set in the front yard and a small boy sitting on the stump of a tree covered with dry ivy, eying them suspiciously.

"Mama's afraid Maria's going to die," the boy said to Prudential.

"Well, she's not," Prudential said. "Dr. Fielding's come with medicine."

The boy, a small-boned, thin boy about four, squinted his eyes and looked up at Helen. "Does it taste terrible?"

"I haven't tasted it," Helen said, "but it's a very good medicine however it tastes."

"Maria will throw up if it doesn't taste good," the boy said.

Maria was a small fragile child, thin like her brother, but she seemed less ill than frightened. Helen sat on the side of the bed and took her pulse, looking down her throat, and at the size of her pupils, her ears, listening to her chest. Her heart was normal, her lungs clear. She left the medication with instructions not to sleep lying down and to drink clear liquids.

"I hear Bea died today," Mrs. Walker said to Prudential as they prepared to leave.

"At twelve forty-eight," Prudential said.

"Before you came?" Mrs. Walker asked Helen coolly.

"She was dead when I arrived. I would've been too late in any case," Helen added, distressed that she felt it necessary to defend herself. "The medication is only successful if you start it before the bacteria attack the respiratory system."

"Did you get Maria in time?" Mrs. Walker asked crisply.

"I'm sure we did," Helen said, shaking Mrs. Walker's hand, following Prudential to the front door. At the door, Mrs. Walker asked Prudential about Sophie.

"Have you heard from her?" Mrs. Walker asked.

Prudential shrugged. "Nothing."

"Nothing?"

Prudential shook her head.

"That's odd, isn't it?"

"I don't know what's odd," Prudential said, walking down the front steps with Helen.

"Did Maria throw up?" the boy, still sitting on the tree stump, asked.

"Not yet," Helen said cheerfully.

The O'Connors, sitting close together next to their daughter's bed, seemed not much older than Laura, who was eleven.

"I didn't go to work today," Mr. O'Connor said, leaning against his wife. "I couldn't."

"He works at the library," Mrs. O'Connor said. "He's the janitor."

"Also at the public grammar school," Mr. O'Connor said. He stood up to let Helen use the chair beside his daughter and she knelt on it, leaning over the fevered girl. "Perhaps we could use cold towels," she said to Prudential. She took out a hypodermic. "This is going to be a little pinprick," she said, "but it will make you feel better by dinnertime."

Mrs. O'Connor was crying when Helen turned around.

"I can't help it," she said, wringing her skirt in her hands.

Helen took out a bottle of erythromycin. "We think this illness is a bacterial infection called legionella but we don't have the confirmed reports yet from the lab. If it is, this will work." She measured out a teaspoon. "Two teaspoons four times a day starting now and going through the night, waking her up every four hours," she said. "Clear liquids, at least one glass every hour." She wiped Laura O'Connor's head and arms and hands with the wet terry cloth towel. "I'm telling everyone to boil their water before you use it. I'll be back tomorrow," she said, laying her hand against the girl's face.

"Thank you, Doctor," Mrs. O'Connor said as Helen left. "We almost died of worry today after we heard about Bea."

"You must be exhausted, Prudential," Mr. O'Connor said. "Up day and night, I hear from David."

"I don't tire easy," Prudential said matter-of-factly, smoothing her cotton uniform with a long-fingered hand dark with age.

"Have you heard from Sophie?" Mrs. O'Connor asked.

"No," Prudential said, opening the front door.

"Nor have I," Mrs. O'Connor said, "and I expected to."

"You never know." Prudential called good-bye to Laura.

"Who is Sophie?" Helen asked as they made their way up the long steep path to the house where Sallie Durham lived at the end of Tea Lane, a dead-end street of old tiny houses, dollhouses.

"She's a woman from this town who left," Prudential said, knocking on the front door of the Durhams' house.

A pretty woman with a lovely open smile answered the door. "You've come for Sallie? It's so nice of you to come." She kissed Prudential on the cheek. "Sallie's better, I think. I'm Ann," she said to Helen, leading her through the brightly decorated narrow house, painted crazily with pinks and yellows, black polka-dotted walls, sunflowers painted alongside the fireplace.

"I'm glad to see you, Pru," Ann Durham said. "I've been wondering how you're doing."

"Same as always," Prudential said. "Same as you."

"And Sophie?"

"Sophie's not in touch."

Helen followed Ann Durham into the bedroom where Sallie sat silent, her eyes unfocused, propped up with pillows, surrounded by stuffed animals as large as she was.

"I don't like doctors," she said, putting a large stuffed rabbit in front of her face.

"You love Prudential, Sal," Ann Durham said.

Sallie shook her head.

Helen leaned over and took the child's pulse, her temperature, listened to her heart.

"I think you're getting better," she said.

Sallie looked at her directly. "I don't like doctors."

"Sallie was premature," Ann Durham said, reaching over to pick Sallie up, but Prudential was already taking her on her lap. "She's seen too many doctors."

"So listen to me, Sallie Durham," Prudential

murmured in the child's ear, rocking her back and forth until she relaxed and let Helen look down her throat, listen to her chest.

"She's still got fever," Helen said, "and some fluid in her chest." She gave Ann Durham the medicine with instructions. "I'll be back early tomorrow to check in," she said, "or call me if there's any problem."

By the time they had finished at Brian Bliss's apartment located above the five-and-ten-cent store on Main Street, Helen was too weary to think clearly but, walking with Prudential in the early dusk, she had a peculiar feeling as if she were a part of a story in which she didn't understand her role. She wanted Prudential to talk to her. She wanted a confidant, a friend. She liked this woman Prudential, liked the size and strength and hard resistance of her. But it was clear that for whatever reason, and there did seem to be one, she wasn't going to talk.

5.

When David Jaspersen arrived at the yellow clapboard house on the road just above the clinic, Helen was asleep sitting on the couch, her feet resting on her luggage, her head dipping toward her chest, a mass of long hair falling out of the hairpins she had stuck in a circle around the bun she wore. The noise he made opening the front door woke her, alarmed her even, and she didn't move, disoriented at first by the unfamiliar place and then by the strangeness of the man standing across the room from her.

"Did I wake you?" he asked.

She brushed her hair out of her eyes.

"Do you remember me?" He laughed.

"I think so." But it took a moment before she did remember where she was: Meridian, Ohio, here as a physician, and this man standing in her living room was the chief of police out of uniform.

"You changed clothes," she said.

"I'm off duty." He sat down on a large overstuffed chair across from her. "It's almost nine."

"At night?" She looked outside at the silver dusk of May. "Oh, brother."

"People have called. The O'Connors, I think, and Edith Winters, the minister's wife, came by to take you to dinner."

"I didn't hear anything," she said.

"They knocked, they said, but you must have been sound asleep," he said. "I'm sorry I'm late."

She stood up, pushing her bags out of the way. Her legs were stiff, weak-kneed, the blood running too thick. "I'm hungry. I feel as if I'll die if I don't eat something."

"I brought something for dinner," he said. "Pasta and some wine. I'll cook."

He'd left the grocery bag on the front step and she followed him while he retrieved it, followed him to the kitchen, which was small and painted a soft peach color with white cabinets and a square farm table in the corner of the room, a vase of yellow freesias in the middle.

"Is this the place where the other doctor lived?" she asked, sitting on one of the ladder-back chairs.

"It is," David said. "He lived here alone with his cat, who is probably someplace in the fields out back. I feed him."

"This doesn't seem like the kind of place for a man to live alone," she said. "It's more like a woman's place."

"Richard Hazelton has an eye for pretty things."

"Did you bring the flowers?" she asked, playing with the petals of the freesias beside her.

"Edith did," he said, filling a pot with water, turning on the stove.

"Wine?"

She nodded.

He poured her a glass of white wine and put it on the table.

"Why did the other doctor leave?" she asked.

"We don't know," David said, taking a jar of marinara sauce out of the bag, a loaf of French bread. "One day he was simply gone with a note that said he had suddenly been called out of town. Then he wrote to say that he wouldn't be returning for some time."

"You all are full of secrets here, aren't you?"

Helen said, folding her legs under her, resting her chin in her hand.

"Not really," David said, tasting the marinara sauce bubbling on the top of the stove. "Until Maggie Sailor disappeared, nothing happened here."

"Except you had a television film made about you."

"That certainly happened," David said, taking a saucepan for the pasta, washing the lettuce. "I have the cassette in case you didn't see the film when it aired two weeks ago."

At dinner, across the farm table from David, Helen brought up Sophie.

"Sophie?" David asked, pouring himself a second glass of wine.

"When I was making house calls today, every family asked Prudential about Sophie."

"And what did Prudential say?"

"She said she hadn't heard from Sophie." Helen took seconds on pasta and finished the marinara sauce. "Who is she?"

"Sophie DeLaurentis," David said. "Pru didn't tell you?"

Helen shook her head. "Prudential has nothing to say about anything."

David laughed, getting up to take the French bread out of the oven. "She is close to the vest," he said.

"Actually," Helen said, "she did say something. She said that Sophie had left town."

"That's correct."

"You have a lot of trouble with people suddenly leaving town, don't you?"

David shook his head, a look of bemusement on his face, a sweet look, not confrontational, but he wasn't going to talk about Sophie either except to say that it wasn't so odd Sophie leaving town, she was a fly-by-night woman with little staying power.

There was a meow and David opened the door to a large sleek black and white cat with a bow tie on his mouth and a white tail. "This is Gregory," he said.

The cat walked across the room, his tail perpendicular, swatting at the air. He stopped at Helen and hopped into her lap.

"I hope you like cats."

She shrugged.

"He comes with the house," David said.

After dinner David showed her the house. "Edith cleaned yesterday," he said. "Dr. Hazelton left absolutely nothing except cat food. Even the refrigerator was empty, although he was so thin we used to joke that he lived on antibiotics." This seemed to amuse him. He opened the closet doors. "I see she got you hangers," he said.

The bathroom cupboard had two sets of kelly-green towels with the price tags still on, freesias in the bathroom too; the bedroom was large, almost the full size of the house, with an old painted wooden desk in the window, a double four-poster bed with a blue plaid quilt and starched white pillows up against the headboard, a hanging basket of lavender geraniums in the south window. In the corner of the room was a rocking horse, not a very old one, although the paint was chipped, especially on the bright red saddle, and an old-fashioned doll with a china face dressed in an organdy pinafore, her pink plaster feet unshod, sat on the floor under a window. "I don't know where the doll came from. Not Dr. Hazelton," he said. "Maybe one of Edith's whimsies." He turned on the hall light and she followed him downstairs. "So there you are."

"It's very nice," she said but she was thinking that in Ann Arbor, when the job for a visiting physician was first advertised, there was mention of a three-bedroom house and this house was tiny, with only a living room and kitchen and bedroom above them both. She didn't want to complain, in fact was very pleased to be in this small house with the added company of a black and white cat, but she did wonder, without mentioning it to David Jaspersen, why they should say a three-bedroom house when the house had only one. Did they think it would be so difficult to find a visiting physician without the offer of a large house?

"This street doesn't have a name," David was saying, "but it dead-ends on the top of the hill and you are the second house from Main Street, then, going up, is the pharmacist's house and then the older brother of Mr. Rubin and then

T. J. Wisely's house, although why he wants to go up and down that hill in a wheelchair I don't know." He sat back down in the living room. "You know which one T. J. is?"

"I do," Helen said.

"Women find him handsome."

"He came by the clinic today."

"Looking for Prudential?" he asked. "They're very close. She practically raised him." He told Helen about T. J.'s arrival in Meridian, about Prudential, how she had come, maybe in her fifties, from Washington, D.C., where she had been working in a good government job, perhaps on the staff of a senator, he thought, but she had gone to Harrisville, Ohio, with a schoolteacher whom she called her husband but he wasn't, and when he died Prudential moved to Meridian and took a house and a job in the clinic as a nurse, keeping her counsel about her life and business.

"If you'd like to see the film," he said, "Ben Winters brought over that television and a VCR."

"I'd like to see it later," Helen said, sinking into the couch.

"I know you're exhausted."

"You don't have to leave though," she said, feeling a sudden melancholy, wanting him to stay for a while, maybe spend the night—he could sleep on top of the blue and white quilt in the bedroom and then he would be there in the event of an emergency, and though of course she didn't mention to him what she was thinking, it seemed to her a reasonable request. Which was the way her romances often began, quickly with a safe stranger, a fellow student, a physician, a person with whom she had no history, whose own personal history was reliable. She wasn't a woman who gave the impression of need but she knew she was starved for a kind of animal comfort, a physical proximity exempt from matters of the heart. She didn't want to spend a night alone in Dr. Hazelton's pristine and impersonal house. "Would you like to spend the night?" she could say. "I'm accustomed to someone spending the night. I have a small fear of being alone," she could tell him, "especially now, back in Meridian, this place to which I haven't returned since Emma died. Which means that the last time I walked these streets and smelled this peculiar river smell she was alive."

"I have a son," he said.

"I didn't know that you were married," she said.

"I'm not any longer," he said. "But I have a son."

She took the pins out of her hair so it fell to her shoulders, slipped on her shoes. "I suppose you ought to leave then since you have responsibilities," she said. "It's awfully late."

"I do need to leave," he said, showing her where the telephone was, writing down his home number and the number of the Winters house. "If anything comes up, call me. I live only half a mile away."

She walked with him to the door feeling a kind

of yearning from childhood, wishing her mother with her, in the room forever.

"In the last three weeks since the film aired people come here as tourists just to see the things they saw on television, although I can't imagine why," he said. His arm against the door, he brushed her hair off her forehead. "In the future, you'll be able to say that you were a doctor in a famous town."

She wanted to tell him she'd been in Meridian as a child but something kept her from saying it, as if her childhood here, of which, until her last visit, she had nothing but sweet memories, might be exposed as something else.

She leaned against the wall, thinking of a way to detain him. "When I was small, I used to be out of the blue lonely; my mother told me that happens with only children."

"I'm an only child too, an only child of elderly parents now dead," David said, confidentially as if there were something not only in common, but exchanged between them, a bartered piece of heart.

"My parents are alive," Helen said, "but we're estranged." She wanted to tell him about Emma, who was crowding her mind.

"I know about estrangement," David said and the remark, the way he said it, was provocative, somehow even romantic.

It was odd, Helen thought later, how small paragraphs of personal stories took on a momentum, propelled a person forward into a territory without parameters.

The first tenet of medicine is "Do no harm." *Do no harm,* Dr. Covington had said in the initial meeting of Human Biology in her first year of medical school. "You must remember that whenever you are dealing with a human life: 'Do no harm.' "

But how was it possible to avoid harm if her own nerve center was in cold storage? Helen had asked herself, slipping out of one relationship into a new one without a change of step. She didn't want another love affair to call to her attention that at some part of herself, some central part essential to living, she couldn't be stirred.

She didn't sleep well in Dr. Hazelton's high pencil-post double bed. She fell in and out of consciousness, turning back and forth, unable to settle. But she was asleep when the phone rang beside her bed and she knocked it off the cradle trying to answer.

"Prudential?" a man's voice said.

"This isn't Prudential," Helen answered.

"What number is this then?" he asked crossly.

"I'm not sure," she said, turning on the light. "This is Helen Fielding," she said. "I've just moved here."

"I'm sorry," the man said. "I must have dialed the wrong number."

Afterward, Helen couldn't sleep. She turned

on the light and got up, checking the list of numbers the chief of police had given her, checking the number on her telephone. 693-0468. She dialed her mother in New York City and hung up before it rang.

The bedroom was cold and damp. She took a sweater out of her bag, climbed back in bed, opened *Anna Karenina* and she must have fallen asleep then. When she woke up, it was dawn, she was still sitting with the light on beside her bed and someone was banging at the front door.

6.

Sallie Durham struggled for breath. Her tiny face was blue, her eyes rabbit wide in terror and she was dying.

"She's dying, isn't she?" Ann Durham hung on the back of Helen, pulled at the neck of her sweater.

"Leave the doctor alone, Ann," Sam Durham said evenly. "Please, Annie, leave her be."

"She's going, I can see it," Ann Durham said. "Tell me she isn't."

"Hush, Annie," Sam Durham said.

"Promise me she won't."

Someone took Ann Durham away, perhaps Sam Durham, perhaps someone else because the Durham house was full of people when Helen arrived just before seven in the morning. "They all came out of their houses with Annie's screaming," Sam Durham had said, rushing ahead, bringing Helen through the house to the back room, too damp and cold for a sick child to be lying in.

"Would someone call Prudential?" Helen asked.

"Prudential," one man said. "You go get her."

"Doesn't she have a phone?"

"I'll call," someone said.

"I'll call," another said.

And in the background, maybe the next room, Annie Durham was crying.

Helen was left alone with the child, losing consciousness, lying in a circle of dampness on her pale blue crib sheet, the morning light through a dirt-streaked window dappled like measles across her face.

She felt the child's throat, just below the Adam's apple, took the small scalpel from her medical bag and in a swift movement made a small incision and inserted a tube, connecting the tube to oxygen.

"Prudential's not there," she heard someone say.

And then, probably Sam Durham behind her, "Prudential doesn't answer her phone."

No one could say why so many people had gathered early in the morning at the Durhams' house, crowding into the living room, the dining room filling up with food on the long table, coffeecakes and doughnuts, toast and jam and Danish, thick, sweet comforting pastries brought in by neighbors who came, some just out of bed, their hair uncombed. The street outside was lined with people, brimming with conversation, carrying coffee in Styrofoam cups from Aunt Amy's coffee house—not a gladiator crowd, the kind at the scene of accidents, pulling at the ropes of human consciousness. But not necessarily a generous crowd either. There was an uneasy feeling of accumulated terror in the air—the last straw for a town unacquainted with collective trouble, selected by the god of bad news to be at the eye of the storm.

"Would you like a cup of coffee?" Sam Durham asked Helen but she shook her head.

"Not yet," she said.

He seemed a nice man and she liked the desperate way he tried to save his daughter by good behavior, maintaining a steady calm, asking after Helen's needs, apologizing for his wife's remarks.

"She's lost her head, I'm afraid," Mr. Durham said. "She doesn't mean what she says."

"Don't worry," Helen said.

Prudential didn't arrive and David Jaspersen had left for Harrisville, where a truck had overturned on a small car.

"Does anyone here have Emergency Medical Training in case I need help?" Helen asked Sam Durham, who came back with the information that three of the people waiting for news were members of the volunteer ambulance service.

After the IV was in, Helen moved the child's bed away from the window, washed her face, her plump hands, brushed the damp yellow curls plastered to her forehead, and waited, standing over the crib, her arms folded across her chest, watching.

"I wonder where Prudential might be," she asked the next time Sam Durham came in.

"Someone says she's at T. J. Wisely's," he said. "Something happened to T. J. in the middle of the night but he doesn't answer his phone, so no one knows. Sometimes he falls."

"It's almost eight o'clock," Helen said. "She ought to be at work soon."

"Prudential lives by her own clock," Sam Durham said, moving a little closer to the crib. "What do you think?"

"I don't know yet."

"Can Ann come in now?"

Helen shook her head.

"She's too upset," she said. "We have to wait to see how things go. Sallie looks a little better."

The child's eyes were open, her pupils dilated, her eyes fixed on Helen. She was a particularly small and delicate child, perfectly proportioned with a broad forehead and large oval-shaped black eyes, like the eyes on the plump-bellied cupids with tiny wings floating across late Renaissance paintings.

Helen reached over and touched her hair, dry

now with a life of its own, yellow curls springing to attention even as her body threatened to shut down.

Days after Emma died or maybe it was months later—time had a way of scattering—Helen had an intact memory of an afternoon lunch at her grandmother's in Michigan with lemon meringue pie and the faint smell of honeysuckle in the air.

"I've got work to do for my graduate classes this afternoon," her father was saying to her mother. "I think I'll go to the library."

"And I should pack to go back to Ann Arbor tomorrow morning," her mother said.

"What about you, Helen?" her grandmother asked. "I ought to know a little girl to invite over to play. Maybe the Summers' child."

"I don't want to play with a little girl," Helen said, and this she remembered clearly because she wasn't a child given to taking emotional risks. "I only want to play with Emma."

The weight of the afternoon dropped on her shoulders. The pale lemon pie left barely touched on her plate grew to enormous proportions, the bodies of the grownups spread across the table in a tidal wave, smothering her until she couldn't breathe.

"Excuse me," her father said and left.

Her mother folded her napkin and stood up.

"Excuse me," her grandmother said, pushing back her chair.

And Helen was left with the sound of her own voice speaking her sister's name.

"Prudential's here," Sam Durham said from the doorway.

Helen turned around.

Prudential was dressed in her nurse's uniform, a white cap perched cockily on her head and a MERIDIAN HIGH SCHOOL sweatshirt tied around her narrow waist. She carried an umbrella although there was no evidence of rain.

"You need me here?" Prudential asked. She walked over to the bed and looked down at Sallie Durham. "Uh-huh," she made a sound in her throat.

"I need you to go to the clinic," Helen said. "I'm staying here for a while."

She walked with Prudential to the door.

"What are all of these people doing here?" Helen asked, looking beyond the front door of the Durhams' house.

Prudential shook her head.

"I don't know," she said.

"I feel as if I'm being scrutinized." Helen folded her arms across her chest.

"You could be," Prudential said without sympathy. "People might be hanging around to see if you're going to bring a miracle or not."

She was a handsome woman with unlined dark skin and eyes too black to see the pupils, a distinguished face, large for the fineness of her long willowy body.

"Is Sallie Durham going to live?" she asked.

"I don't know," Helen said. "I just can't say for sure."

"I'll call from the clinic if there's an emergency," Prudential said.

"Do you have the number?"

"I know every number in Meridian," Prudential said.

"Well, someone in Meridian doesn't know yours because he called in the middle of last night asking to speak with you."

"He found me," Prudential said, swinging her umbrella around like a cane, nodding hello to people as she walked through the small crowd.

Sam Durham pulled a straight-back chair over and sat with Helen in the room, crossing his long legs, resting his elbows on the bed. "You're worried about Sallie?" He was tentative. "Is that why you're staying here so long?"

"I'm less worried than I was," she said.

"I sent Annie over to her mother's for a couple of hours," he said. "Her nerves are bad."

They sat side by side, the morning sun through the window warming their backs, his presence so comfortable that Helen began to wonder had she known him, had he been one of the little boys who spun around on a two-wheeler in front of Aunt Martha's house when she was young or went with her and her father to the drugstore for a double-dip chocolate soda at the counter on thick summer afternoons.

This past year living with Oliver, she had been lonely, struck by the oddness of such isolation in his company. Sometimes she sat up in bed after a particularly long day on the pediatric floor, looking at the pictures in her home magazines, feeling abandoned. She would touch Oliver's sculpted hand to see if it was real. He seemed an unwieldy mannikin in the bed beside her and, though he was a man of British reserve with a surgeon's absence of communication, he was not without force in her life and the loneliness surprised her.

Oliver had a fondness for games and puzzles, jigsaw puzzles in particular, and he kept a large one of fish at one end of the dining-room table, bass and trout, bluefish and scrod, doing a bit of it each night before he went to bed and, when it was completed, undoing it and starting over. For his birthday this past year she had sent a picture of herself to a company she found in the back of *Country Living* which made large jigsaw puzzles from photographs. During the spring, the fish on the dining-room table were replaced by jigsaw bits of Helen Fielding, the corner of a blue eye, shape after shape of brown hair, bits of flesh. Sometimes she worried that she was losing her mind as she watched Oliver sitting at a straight-back chair at the end of the dining-room table, his fine-boned hand moving a piece of jigsaw around the half-shaped reproduction of her face.

"Did you grow up here?" she asked Sam Durham.

"I did," he said. "I left for college but when my father died I came home and took his job." He reached over and touched his daughter's hand.

"Did you ever know Martha Fowler?"

"She was my aunt," he said.

"She was your aunt?" Helen asked, a lump gathering in her throat.

He nodded. "My aunt by marriage," he said. "You knew her?"

"I did," she said. "I knew her when I was little."

"So you've been here before?" he asked.

She didn't reply, turning her attention to the child.

She checked Sallie's pulse, her chest, her temperature. Her temperature had broken. Her breathing was less labored. She didn't want to pursue this conversation with Sam Durham. She wasn't sure why she had decided to keep her relationship to Meridian secret, but instinctively she had, as if to tell put her at risk.

"You know Sallie is in the film," Sam Durham said. "Have you seen it?"

"I haven't," she said. "I've heard about it, of course."

"They have a lot of shots of Sallie. The director

liked her," he said. "Her and Molly. They were his favorites."

"Molly?" Helen asked, flattening the thin yellow blanket over Sallie, checking the IV. She looked up. "I haven't met Molly."

Mr. Durham's face darkened. "Of course," he said. "You wouldn't have met her." There was something peculiar in the way he said it, as if he had surprised himself bringing up her name.

"Who is Molly?" Helen asked Prudential when she arrived back at the clinic just after noon, Sallie Durham out of immediate danger, the crowd in front of the Durhams' house dispersed with the demands of the day.

"Molly?" Prudential looked up from the desk where she was writing on a chart. "I don't know about Molly," she said, taking her cap off, scratching the top of her head with a pencil. "You had a call from the O'Connors," she said. "The medicine is working."

III.
Heart Scan

The Story of

MERDIAN

Tuesday, April 10

Peter Forester had the reputation of a gifted film director with an eye for the small detail which in its particular describes the whole—like the stopped clock or the crop of hair that fell beneath David Jaspersen's police cap, giving his strong-featured face a vulnerability, or Sophie DeLaurentis's eyes, not large but round, almost perfectly round. The camera caught her straight on looking exactly at the viewer, canceling the landscape. He filmed her in the small garden behind her house, brushing away the debris of winter, exposing the tiny shoots of daffodils, on the front steps with Molly—a frame in which Molly picked up her mother's hand and kissed the fingers—at the playground and the market, buying round pink plush curlers at the pharmacy. Somehow the sight of her soft face checking the selection of hair curlers had a surprising innocence. There was a frame of Sophie and Molly sharing a milkshake at the counter of the ice cream store with Ann and Sallie Durham when David Jaspersen came in with the news that Mona Dickenson had died of liver cancer, earlier than had been expected, giving the film crew an opportunity to make a record of grief.

"It makes a difference that the woman was young," Peter Forester said to T. J. later.

"What do you mean?" T. J. asked.

"She was young and a woman," Peter said. "Heartbreak combination."

"Mona sold tickets at the movies when I was in junior high," T. J. said. "She had the longest legs I've ever seen on a girl. I used to watch the movie imagining her with me."

"Listen, T. J.," Peter said. "To shoot a film in your hometown was your idea; there's no room for sentimentality. Pay attention to the goal and forget the particulars."

The method Peter Forester selected was documentary, filming the town day to day with a kind of randomness, up and down the streets, in the shops, the clinic where Prudential was, at the schools and the churches, inside the houses, along the river. Peter had favorites, not like Sophie but favorites all the same, and there was more footage of David Jaspersen and Prudential and Ann Durham and Mrs. Gunn, whose husband had drowned in one of the floods. Molly DeLaurentis was a favorite and Sallie Durham and Marcie Bliss, who had been born with a clubfoot, and Marcie's Uncle Trip, who had played first base with the Cincinnati Reds until he got

Lou Gehrig's disease and lived with the Blisses, writing baseball stories for the Harrisville paper.

"I want to begin with the river," Peter told T. J. and the film crew the morning of the second day, sitting in the front booth of Shirley's Cafe. "Starting north of town where the river is narrow, moving right up as the water widens south to the railroad station."

"Maybe we should have waited a couple of weeks to see if we have a flood this year," T. J. said. "It's the floods that bring this town together."

Peter shook his head. "We can have the illusion of floods," he said. "Television has too much high drama. We're after the genuine in 'Meridian.' "

T. J. was in David Jaspersen's office when David came back with his lunch from Shirley's.

"You aren't who I was hoping to see," David said, checking the list of phone calls which had come in.

"I've come with an emergency." T. J. opened the desk drawer. "No cigarettes?"

"No cigarettes."

He took out a pack of matches and two quarters. "For a Coke," he said.

"What is the emergency?" David asked.

"Sophie is taking this seriously," T. J. said. "She thinks she's a movie star."

"She is," David said. "She's got a camera following her around all day and that handsome small-scale giraffe Forester you've imported from the city of our dreams hanging on her words as if they counted for something near gospel importance. What do you expect?"

"I want you to talk to Peter Forester, David," T. J. said. "I want you to tell him that Sophie isn't really from Meridian and that to have so much of her puss on the screen contradicts the whole point of the film. Right?" he asked nervously. "Don't you think so?"

"I'm not thinking about this film," David said. "It's happening and my job is to keep the town in order."

"Christ, David," T. J. said. "You know what I'm talking about. I'm going a little crazy," he said.

David shrugged.

"It's like we're one of those towns zapped by radiation and we poor dopes haven't got a clue that the camera is shooting invisible poisons."

"If you're so worried about Sophie, tell her. Tell her to clip the wings of her new-found acting career and pay attention to what's valuable in life," David said. "I'm sure she'll be grateful for your help."

"Is that the full extent of your advice?"

"It is," David said. "You know Mona Dickenson died this morning?"

"I heard," T. J. said. "Peter Forester wants to film the funeral."

David shook his head in disbelief. "Film the funeral?"

"He's grateful for the chance to shoot a real-life tragedy."

David sat down at the desk and picked up the telephone. "I have about ten calls to make, T. J. I have to go to the Dickensons' house and to the clinic because a pipe burst in the bathroom and to the grammar school for a meeting with Win's teacher and to court in Harrisville on a robbery at three, all the time keeping my hair combed so I'll look good in your movie." He took the receiver off the cradle and dialed. "I can't worry about Sophie DeLaurentis today."

T. J. flung his head back against the wall, put his hand splayed across his face and when he spoke his voice had a mannered and unnatural quality as if he were imitating the voice of a woman.

"I believe in this film, David. I love Meridian but something in the way Peter Forester is going about it is making me insane."

When T. J. was young, after he lived with the Jaspersens and had moved on to the Wades and the Dickensons and then the Flowers, before Prudential came to town and took him in, he followed David Jaspersen everywhere. He copied the way he dressed, in heavy boots and jeans belted at the waist and wool plaid shirts tucked in, the way he walked, one shoulder lower than the other, a swagger to his hips, his hair kept washed and cut, unlike the hair of the other boys in high school in Meridian.

But after David's parents died, one after the other, of cancer in his junior year of high school, David took after T. J. in a mean way. "Leave me alone," he said. "I don't want to be bothered by you. Drop off the earth."

And he felt bad about that, especially since T. J. Wisely was the only young person in Meridian who knew what it was like to be without parents, first in line for trouble. And so through the years they had developed a closeness as if they knew things other people did not know.

When T. J. headed up Main to join the crew after lunch, Sophie was sitting at the lunch counter of Shirley's, Molly on her lap and Peter Forester right beside her, his thin hip against her flesh, laying claim.

T. J. pushed open the door and wheeled inside.

"Sophie?"

"Hiya, T. J.," Sophie said, turning Molly to face T. J. "Say hi to T. J., Molly."

"Hiya," Molly said.

Shirley's was crowded with citizens hoping for bit parts in "The Story of Meridian," walk-ons, crowd shots. There was a spirit of conviviality. Peter's assistant Marina was sitting next to him smoking a long European cigarette and Pleeper Jones was behind the camera set up in the rear of the diner next to the rest room.

"Sophie," T. J. called. "C'n I speak to you a minute?"

"I'm shooting her, T. J.," Peter called. "Give me a second to set up."

Molly hopped down from her mother's lap and wandered over to T. J., swinging her small arms. She was a classic eighteenth-century child whose wide-browed face and gray eyes had an enchanting solemnity. This afternoon she had been dressed by Sophie for the occasion in an organdy pinafore over a yellow smocked dress which, because of its starchiness, she didn't like to wear and squirmed, pulling at the shoulders.

"Hi, T. J.," she said, standing in front of him, her hand on the arm of his wheelchair.

"Climb up," T. J. said.

She scrambled onto his lap and sat with her plump legs out straight in front of her.

"I want to see your eye," she said earnestly, reaching toward the black eye patch covering his left eye.

"You see my eye," he said. "It's green with yellow flecks."

"I want to see the other eye hiding."

"That eye?" he asked softly. "Are you sure?"

She nodded, folding her hands in her lap.

T. J. reached up to the black patch and lifted it, exposing an empty socket with a thin transparent lid closed over the small space.

Molly caught her breath.

"See?" he said. "No eye."

She raised her hands and covered her eyes.

"I didn't think you'd like it," T. J. said.

She bent her head so she could only see the

white organdy pinafore between the spaces her fingers made.

"Molly?"

She didn't reply.

"Look, Molly, I've put the patch back."

But she didn't look up.

"It's okay, Molly." He touched her hair. "The eye hole is gone."

But as he reached under her arms to lift her off his lap she screamed, a long thin ribbon of sound.

When Molly started screaming, Dr. Richard Hazelton, between patients at the clinic, had just come into the rear of Shirley's for lunch. He made his way behind Pleeper Jones and his camera toward the front of the diner, a tall, visibly restrained young man, pale-skinned with soft straight blond hair, thin, too thin, almost unwell-seeming except that he moved with an athletic grace.

"What is going on?" he asked Pleeper.

"Beats me," Pleeper said. "T. J. seems to have created a scene."

"T. J.," Dr. Hazelton said, breaking through the crowd, "what's going on?"

Sophie had already picked up Molly, who wrapped her arms around her mother's neck and hid her face in Sophie's shoulder.

"She wanted to see my eye," T. J. said.

"Poor T. J.," Sophie said to Molly. "He got his eye poked out when he had a terrible fall."

Molly shook her head back and forth, her eyes covered with her plump hands, inconsolable.

"She asked to see what was under T. J.'s eye patch," Sophie said to Richard Hazelton.

"She begged," T. J. said with irritation. "She insisted. So I showed her."

"Don't worry, T. J.," Sophie said. "Children are weird."

"It's nothing so awful to look at," T. J. said. "Just different."

"It's no wonder she's upset with all these television people unsettling our lives," Dr. Hazelton said, stroking her hair.

"I'm sorry, Richard," T. J. said. "I'm sorry about the TV."

"Things have a way of getting out of hand," Dr. Hazelton said.

"But I love the television show," Sophie said. "It's the best thing that's happened since I came to Meridian."

Molly had stopped crying. She tightened her arms around her mother's neck and opened her eyes, looking at T. J.

"I want to talk to you about the television show, Sophie," T. J. said.

"Please, T. J.," Sophie said, laying her hand on his cheek. "I'm having such a nice time, I don't want it to stop."

"Someone will pay for this showing off," Dr. Hazelton said quietly and to no one in particular.

"Hello, T. J.," Molly said tentatively. And

then she put one small hand over her own eye, covering it. "My eye is hiding too," she said.

7.

Madeleine Sailor came into the clinic just before three and sat in a straight-back chair by the front door, a beige cardigan pulled across her shoulders although the afternoon was warm for May.

"Have you come to see the doctor, Madeleine?" Prudential asked. "Do you want to sign in?"

Madeleine shook her head.

"I'll wait," she said.

The clinic was crowded, mostly children sitting at the table in the center of the room with games and books and Fisher Price figures, or leaning against their mothers' arms, their eyes half closed or across their mothers' laps. Brian Bliss was there with his grandfather, holding a matchbox car in his tight fist, and Maria Walker sat with her brother on a small couch, pushing him every time his arm or leg crossed the divide between them.

"I'll wait until everyone has seen her," Madeleine said to Prudential. "I'm not sick."

"She's sick whether she knows it or not," Prudential said to Helen, late in the afternoon after hours of sick children and strep tests and blood tests and thermometers and children in underwear, their legs dangling from the examining table, their expressions solemn.

Since the epidemic began, the clinic had been short on everything—clean paper for the examining tables, the plates for strep tests, alcohol; the erythromycin supply was gone by three, no penicillin or cotton balls or sterile gauze. Maria Walker's cousin Amos came in with a sprained wrist from falling off his skateboard and there were no splints and no Ace bandages.

But as the day progressed, Helen began to feel a lightheaded certainty. She was at a hardship post, out of the United States, a third world country, without supplies or access to them, without hospitals or other physicians. What came to pass was up to her in this back country.

She had never worked as a physician in her own right, always as an assistant following another doctor on rounds, but now she had begun to feel the rush she had remembered as a young child playing at being grown up. She liked having her own nurse, this substantial woman. She actually felt a love for Prudential as if they had worked together agreeably for years and against odds, as if they were friends.

She liked her office—she'd get flowers for the long south window tomorrow, she thought, perhaps a dhurrie rug—another desk, rectangular and less forbidding than the huge mahogany box behind which she sat speaking to the parents after she had examined their children, giving them a lollipop or plastic car or barrette for good behavior.

It was almost five when the waiting room finally thinned and Prudential opened the office door.

"Madeleine Sailor is still here," she said, folding her arms across her chest. "Do you know who she is?"

Helen hesitated.

"You saw the poster of the missing child at the train station?"

"I know about the missing child."

"This is her mother."

"I remember," Helen said. "I met her when I arrived."

Prudential put her hand on her hip.

"You may not be familiar with small towns where people know each other by more than name."

"I grew up on an island," Helen said.

"Then you know you can't believe everything you hear."

Madeleine Sailor was nervous. She sat down in the chair across from Helen, sat very straight, her hands clutching a lavender crocheted bag in her lap, and from the angle where Helen was sitting, it looked as if one side of her face was trembling. She was a slender woman, pretty but hollow-faced and pale-skinned. She could have been beautiful in the flush of health. She carried herself with a presence of someone who has been beautiful once.

"I'm the mother of the child who disappeared after the film crew left Meridian," she said in a speech which seemed rehearsed.

"I remember," Helen said, "I'm so sorry," and she immediately wished she had said nothing, had waited for the woman to deliver her own message, undiminished by Helen's small condolences.

"You know about the film 'The Story of Meridian'?" she asked.

"I know about it," Helen replied. "I haven't seen it."

"CBS people came to Meridian to film us in our daily lives," she said. "The director had been looking for a town in America reminiscent of the way towns used to be and T. J.—have you met T. J.?"

"I have." Helen poured a glass of water for herself and one for Madeleine Sailor.

"T. J. grew up here," she said. "He actually lived with my family for a while until Prudential came to town and took him in."

"I've met him," Helen said. "I know he's working hard to find your daughter."

"He is," Madeleine said, opening her purse, taking out a Kleenex which she didn't use but twisted into little balls, lining them up on the desk in front of her. "T. J. knew the director and recommended Meridian," she said.

"It's a very pretty town," Helen said. "I can understand that he would have."

"The director had a particular fondness for some people in the community. Not us. The only shot of me is with Maggie, standing in line outside a funeral wake." She picked up one of the tiny balls of Kleenex, rolling it between her fingers. "I used to smoke," she said, apologetic. "And then when the film crew left—I think it was April 13," she said, "Meridian had changed."

"How?" Helen asked, leaning forward at her desk.

"Just changed," Madeleine said. "We no longer seemed to wish each other well. In fact," she said, "in the past few weeks, we have begun to wish each other ill." She laced her fingers together.

"And on May 10 I was at the drugstore on Main Street and Maggie was waiting outside. That was perfectly normal in Meridian—nothing out of the ordinary has ever happened here. We didn't lock our doors." Her face was gray and certainly trembling. "When I came out of the drugstore it was maybe six o'clock at night and she was gone." She sat unnaturally still. She had probably made a determination not to belittle the gravity of her situation by tears.

Outside the long south window behind Helen, the day was turning silver, a light wind had picked up, singing through the barely open door.

Madeleine Sailor opened the crocheted bag and took out a rectangular box.

"This is 'The Story of Meridian,'" she said, putting the box on Helen's desk. "If you don't have a VCR in Dr. Hazelton's house, you can use ours."

Helen reached over and put the film cassette beside her. "There is a VCR," she said. "And as soon as this legionella is under control, I want to see the film."

Madeleine's clear blue eyes were direct. "I'd be grateful if you'd look at it carefully," she said. "You're from the outside and might be able to see something I can't." She stood up to leave.

"Like what?" Helen asked softly.

"Maybe a clue about what happened to Maggie," Madeleine said.

"You don't believe she was taken by a stranger?"

"I don't know," Madeleine said. "I have to know."

After she left, cleaning up her little row of Kleenex balls, taking the water glass and pitcher, attempting a smile of gratitude, Helen shut the door. The telephone rang and she heard Prudential answer in the waiting room. It rang again but she didn't bother to inquire.

She was conscious of her own presence in the room, a kind of mad expansion of herself as if she had to multiply in size against a quicksand force seeking to pull her under.

Something must have gone terribly wrong in Meridian, Ohio.

Prudential knocked.

"They are sending a delivery of erythromycin from Toledo by messenger," she said. "It'll be here by seven but I have to leave."

"I'll wait," Helen said. She looked at her watch. Five-fifteen. "I want to do another round of house calls this evening."

Prudential folded her arms across her chest.

"I can't," she said. "I have obligations."

Helen nodded.

"Unless there's an emergency," she said, and there was a willingness in her voice Helen had not heard before. "A window of opportunity," her father would have said. "You can call me if there's an emergency."

Helen looked up from the chart on which she was writing at Prudential standing in the doorway, tall and slender, her body unwilling to give in to age. She was somehow entirely satisfactory. They would be friends.

She began to mention Madeleine Sailor's visit but Prudential held up a hand to stop her.

"Don't ask me any personal questions," she said, anticipating.

"This isn't personal," Helen said. "I want to know what has happened in Meridian."

"That is a personal question," Prudential said.

8.

The late afternoon was warm and brilliant, the kind of day that seems in its clarity to be permanent. It was still warm at seven in the evening when Helen left for rounds with the new delivery of erythromycin that had arrived from Toledo. But when she finished at the Durhams' house, the temperature had fallen, the wind had picked up, and the trees in the hills above the Durham cottage swished their long skirts. The sky turned suddenly black.

"We don't need rain," Sam Durham said, walking with Helen to the front door.

Helen took the umbrella he offered. "But you've had your flood for this year, haven't you?" she asked. "That's why this epidemic of legionella. I just had a warning issued for everyone to boil the water."

"We did," Sam Durham said. "But it wasn't the kind of flood we sometimes have because there hasn't been enough rain. There could be another."

"I certainly hope not," Helen said, waving good-bye.

In the shadows behind Sam, Ann Durham appeared a ghost on her own front porch. Helen hadn't seen her since the morning when Sallie was so ill.

"Sallie's better," Helen called. "A lot better, I told Mr. Durham. I'll be at home so you can call me there if you need me."

"Say good-bye, Ann," Sam said to his wife loudly enough for Helen to hear him.

Ann Durham folded her arms across her chest and looked out into the evening just beyond Helen.

"I said good-bye," she said to no one in particular, stepping into the light, looking at Helen blankly.

Maria Walker's brother was sitting on the front porch just under the small roof when Helen arrived.

"Papa says we're going to have a flood," he said.

"I hope not," Helen said, stepping over his legs stretched out in front of the door.

"We will," the boy said solemnly, looking at Helen. "You don't look like a doctor," he said. "You look too much like a girl."

"Girls are doctors," Helen said.

"No, they aren't," he said with confidence.

Mrs. Walker was talkative. Maria was much better, she said. The medicine had been a miracle and now if only Timbo, the little boy on the front porch, sickly by nature, didn't get sick, they'd be home free, she said, smiling. She asked about Sallie Durham.

"She was very sick, wasn't she?"

"She was," Helen said, "but she's much better."

Mrs. Walker shook her head.

"I don't like Ann Durham," she said. "We went to high school together and I didn't like her then either. But," she shrugged, "everybody in Meridian pretends to like everybody else." She put a plate of Oreo cookies on the dining-room table. "Timbo," she called. "You can have one too," she said. "Ann thinks her children are better than other children and they aren't. Children are just children, don't you think?"

Helen nodded, taking an Oreo, hoping to make a quick escape.

"The film made her think that," Mrs. Walker said, pouring Timbo a glass of milk. "Sallie was practically the star. Her and Molly." An odd look crossed her face. "You know the film changed Meridian and I was born here so I know." She split a cookie and licked the white icing. "The film made some people more important than others. And then we started to believe what we saw on TV instead of what was right here on our doorstep." She brushed Maria's hair out of her eyes. "Have you seen it?"

"I haven't but Madeleine Sailor gave me a cassette and I may have a chance to look at it tonight."

"You won't see us," Maria's mother said. "We're not in it, except Timbo. There's a shot of the back of Timbo in the line at nursery school and that's it for the Walker family."

"You must be just as glad," Helen said, not knowing what was expected of her. "I'd hate to be on television."

"I'm just as glad," Maria's mother said but she sounded unconvinced.

It was after nine and very dark when Helen got back to her house. The black and white cat lay curled on the mat, rubbing the back of Helen's legs as she opened the front door, pleased to see her. She went inside, dropped her medical bag, her umbrella, a bunch of limp pale yellow stock the Walkers had given her, turned on the lights.

In the shower, she stood with her eyes closed, her arms stretched out in front of her so the water traveled down to the ends of her fingers, pounded on the top of her head. She could organize her mind in compartments. Empty her brain.

"You have the mind of a man," Oliver had told her early in their relationship when he was still fascinated by her elusiveness.

"Is that better or worse than the mind you had expected?" she asked.

"Neither," he said. "It's simply that you don't let one thing spill over into another like the women I've known do."

Helen's mother had told her that as well when she was young, in grammar school, and her early interest in biology expressed itself in small bottles of formaldehyde with fetal pigs and birds and kittens ordered from a laboratory supply store in LaSalle, Illinois, lined up on the windowsill of her bedroom.

"Sometimes you seem like someone else's daughter with all of your dead animals," her mother had said.

"They're not exactly dead," Helen had said. "They were never born."

"It's not only the bottled animals, Helen, although I certainly wish they weren't living with us," her mother had said with some annoyance. "It's the way you have of doing things, the way you organize, like your father does. Like a man."

"Well, I'm not going to grow up to be a man," Helen had said. "So you don't have to worry."

But the quality of mind had been useful. She had, for example, been able to put the burden of Emma's death completely out of her mind for most of her life until these last few weeks when she had started to think about Meridian again.

She got out of the shower, dried her hair, put on jeans and a man's shirt which had belonged to Oliver, tied her wet hair on top of her head, so it flopped carelessly to one side.

It was almost ten o'clock in the evening and the wind outside was howling when she turned on the television and slipped the "The Story of Meridian" cassette into the VCR.

The film opens without any sound but that of water, with a scene along the river as it narrows, its banks lined with bare slender trees, bending like dancers, some uprooted. Then the river widens broad and fast, moving into the town, and the camera moves up the bank to the railroad station. WELCOME TO MERIDIAN.

"Meridian, Ohio, is located in the northwest corner of Ohio. The border of Michigan to its north and Illinois to its west, west of Cleveland, just west of Toledo, a small hilly town with one main street, a square in the middle without a statue—there have been no famous sons of Meridian to cast in stone—just ordinary people living out their lives in a community remarkable by today's standards for its generosity of spirit. It is early on a Monday morning."

The camera follows Main Street from the station, the shops opening along the sidewalks around the square, schoolchildren in heavy jackets and scarfs, book bags on their shoulders, on their way to school in groups of threes and fours. The camera stops to focus on a young boy, perhaps eleven, standing precariously on the curb watching three young giggling girls meander up the street. There are other boys in the background, friends of the one on the curb, egging him on. As the girls pass, the young boy makes a leap, landing in a wide puddle in the street, splashing the girls, who scream and laugh and shout, flying back up the street toward home, perhaps to change their clothes. The camera follows the girls as they are lost in an expansive view of the hills of Meridian peppered with brightly colored houses. The girls disappear in the horizon and the camera moves just beyond the square with its shops to a small peach cottage behind the library, where two little girls sit on the steps of the porch, close together, their snow-suited shoulders touching. The smaller one, a dark serious child, has a doughnut squeezed in her tiny hand. The other child is Sallie Durham. The child with the doughnut takes one of Sallie's hands, brings it to her lips and kisses it. The camera moves beyond the girls to two women standing in the doorway. One is Ann Durham bundled up in a coat. The second is a small, dark, voluptuous woman in a man's robe, her long hair uncombed. The camera focuses on her.

Helen stopped the video and rewound, starting again as the camera focused on the little girls.

Sam Durham had told her that the director of the film liked Sallie and Molly. So that must be Molly, Helen thought. The child whose identity had slipped Prudential's mind.

She didn't recognize the lovely-looking woman in the man's robe.

The two women speak. Ann Durham says she will pick the girls up after play group. The front door shuts and Ann Durham walks down the street away from the camera, holding the hands of the little girls.

"It is a cold morning in early April," the narrator is saying. "The smell of winter is still in the air, of early morning wood fires, of rain." The narrator is a bass with a voice that rolls out of his belly, a strong romantic voice, and Helen, sitting in a large soft chair, her knees drawn up under her chin, her arms wrapped around her legs, was pleased by the sound of him.

She didn't hear the knocking on her door at first and, when she did, the wind was roaring along the front of the house with such a force, it was difficult to distinguish sound from weather.

The door flew out of her hand when she opened it, banging against the inside wall. And there, brightly lit by the outside floodlight, was T. J. Wisely, wet and scrambled, his white polo shirt soaked to the skin, his eye patch askew.

"It's a terrible night," Helen said, helping him move his wheelchair over the lip of the front door.

"Awful," T. J. said, shaking his long black hair. "I was at the Durhams' and couldn't make it up the hill. A tree's down."

"I think I heard it fall," Helen said, running up the steps to the linen closet to get a towel.

"We may lose the electricity if this keeps up," T. J. said to Helen when she came downstairs with a brand-new kelly-green towel still with the price tag on it and dried T. J.'s hair. He took his wet shirt over his head, pulling off the eye patch with the shirt.

"Shit," he said, shaking his shirt with one hand, holding his palm over his eye from where the black patch had fallen.

"Here," Helen said. "I'll get it."

She dried the patch and handed it back to T. J.

"How did your eye happen?" she asked.

"I've never been sure," T. J. said, adjusting the string. "I was a stunt man in Hollywood."

"You told me."

"I was doing a leap between buildings," he said. "There was even a net but it didn't hold when I landed. So my back broke and I lost my eye and came back home to Meridian, my stunt man days kaput." He arranged the eye patch. "The eye gives people the creeps."

"I'm a doctor," Helen said.

"You're still a woman and it makes women sick," he said. "Just the idea of an empty socket. I know." He wheeled toward the kitchen. "I'm dying of thirst."

"I only have juices and milk," Helen said.

"No beer?" He helped himself to a banana from a bowl in the middle of the table.

"No beer."

"Juice is fine," he said, comfortable in Richard Hazelton's house as if he had visited often, opening the fridge, taking a glass from the cupboard, agile for a man without the use of his legs, moving gracefully on his strong arms.

"The place looks nice," he said.

"I was told Dr. Hazelton is a fastidious man."

"He is," T. J. said. "You could lick the floors." He wheeled into the living room, lifting Gregory from the sofa to his lap.

"Were you friends?" Helen asked.

"No, we weren't particular friends," T. J. said. "He was extraordinarily quiet and he was the kind of boy that people make fun of."

"But you seem to know his house."

"We all know each other's houses," T. J. said, stretching, lifting himself off the seat of the chair with his arms. Gregory leaped out of his lap and onto the floor.

Helen slid into the couch beside his wheelchair, tucked her long legs under her.

"What were you watching when I came up?" T. J. asked.

"The film about Meridian," Helen said. "I'd just started."

"Turn it on again," he said, sitting in front of the television.

"Haven't you seen enough of it?" she asked.

"I never do." He reached over and turned off the lamp beside the couch.

"I was here," Helen said, turning the play button so the film showed the back of Ann and Sallie Durham, with a wide-angle lens, followed them down the street toward town, disappearing into the village.

"Who is the second little girl, not Sallie?" Helen asked.

"Molly."

"I haven't met her yet."

"You won't," T. J. said. "She left."

Helen laughed. "A lot of people seem to leave Meridian, don't they?"

"I suppose some do," T. J. replied, giving her an odd look.

* * *

The camera dances up Main Street, skipping from one brightly painted shop to the next, the pharmacist, the dry cleaners, a dress shop, pale lavender, sunflower yellow, blue. Then stops, holding a still picture framed by the hills of Meridian.

"We painted the houses for the film, you know." T. J. lifted himself out of the wheelchair to the couch next to Helen. "When I moved here, it was nice but not a fairy tale place." T. J. shrugged. He took out a cigarette. "Mind?"

"Yes," Helen said. "I mind."

He put the unlit cigarette in his mouth and settled into the couch, lifting one leg across the other, sinking into the pillows.

Helen was comfortable with men. Not flirtatious exactly but soft and accessible with a slow charm as if a man could slip into her life unharmed.

"The clinic comes next," T. J. said. "The camera's going to pick up Ann and Sallie at the top of Main going into the clinic. You'll see Prudential charging up the hill in a second and then Dr. Hazelton."

Ann is carrying Sallie, crossing the road beside the barn-red house where MAGGIE Headquarters is, Prudential flying up the street in a turquoise ski jacket and pumpkin-orange scarf, carrying an umbrella, although it isn't raining, waving the umbrella at Ann Durham.

The camera moves in on the meeting of Ann and Prudential in front of the clinic.

"I'm late, late, late," Prudential is saying cheerily. "I overslept in all this gloomy spring weather we've been having." She picks up Molly.

"Which one of you is sick, girl?" Prudential asks.

"It's Molly," Ann says. "She has a sore throat so I've brought her to get a strep test."

The wind had picked up outside, banging the shutters against the house, sailing past the windows as if it had actual shape. There was a crash next to the house and the telephone rang, a half ring, and cut off.

"A hangup?" Helen said.

"The phones are probably out. It happens a lot," T. J. said. "Could you turn up the volume?" he asked, leaning toward the television, fixated, caught up in the narrative as if he were seeing it for the first time. "I can't hear the television with all the wind."

Prudential is opening the door to the clinic, walking with Molly across the waiting room. In the distance Dr. Hazelton, his back to the camera, is looking through the files.

"Prudential?" he calls.

"Good morning, Dr. Hazelton," Prudential says, taking off her jacket, lifting Molly, setting her on the counter.

"Good morning." His head is bent, he riffles through the file drawer. "I'm looking for Jack O'Brien's file. He broke his arm falling in the shower this morning."

Prudential leans down, takes off Sallie's coat and puts her up next to Molly. The camera moves past Prudential over her amazing head to Dr. Hazelton, who turns slowly, a file in hand, and faces the camera.

"Hello, Ann," he says in a pleasant tenor voice. "Who's feeling badly today?"

"Molly," Ann says. "She's not actually sick. Sophie just wanted to have her throat checked."

Dr. Hazelton walks toward the camera, a tall beanpole of a man, pale, pale thin face, pale hair, an inscrutable expression, perhaps indifference but familiar to Helen in his remarkable paleness.

"So that's Dr. Hazelton," Helen said. "Is he actually that white or is it the TV?"

"He's pretty white," T. J. said. "Look at his arms. Have you ever seen such long arms?"

"I can't tell."

"They almost seem deformed."

The lights flickered then, the images on the television screen scattered and disappeared and the living room went dark.

"I knew this was going to happen," T. J. said.

Helen stared out into the blackness, waiting for her eyes to adjust. "Will it last?" she asked.

"Sometimes hours," T. J. said.

They were sitting at either end of the long couch, their arms slung over the back, their hands almost touching.

"Now what?" Helen asked.

"Now we wait," T. J. said.

They didn't speak. For a long time, long

enough to make Helen self-conscious, they sat in silence and listened to the wind, the strange sound it made of air forced through a narrow tunnel as the storm traveled through Meridian.

"Do you have children?" T. J. asked finally. His voice in the darkness had a different sound to it, a weight like the voice of the narrator on "The Story of Meridian."

"I'm not married," Helen said.

"I was married once for a few months," T. J. said. "To a stunt woman. Her specialty was fires."

Helen laughed.

"No joke," he said. "I don't know what I was thinking."

"I haven't thought of being married before," Helen said, "but I've thought of having a child."

"That's actually why I got married," T. J. said.

In the distance there was a dull bang, maybe a car.

"I hope it's not an accident," T. J. said.

They listened but the sound seemed to be the wind, steady, unfriendly in its persistence.

"Are you afraid?" he asked.

"Of what?" She suddenly felt his proximity.

"Of the storm," he said.

"Of the dark," Helen said. "I grew up on an island in the North and it was dark all winter and there was just my mother and me. She was always afraid of the dark."

"What's she like?" T. J. asked.

"My mother?"

"Yes, your mother."

"She's a painter," Helen said. "She actually makes collages out of things she finds like bird bones and dried flowers and stones. They're quite nice," Helen said, wishing now she had one of her mother's collages. She especially liked one that Allie had offered her when she went away to college called *Birds in Flight.* But the birds were not in flight. There was a large framed box with the brilliant feathers of birds clinging to the branches of trees made of delicate twigs. Real feathers, real twigs and painted birds in black on white with outsized claws gripping the real branches for dear life.

"I mean what is she like as a person?" T. J. asked. "I take an interest in mothers."

"I never see her," Helen said. "She's afraid to travel."

"I had a mother obviously," T. J. said, "but all I remember about her is smells like cinnamon or cheap perfume."

"David told me how you got here on a train from Chicago."

"I can't imagine putting a child on a train to a place you've found on a map," he said, "but that's what she did."

"Parents do awful things with children," Helen said, suddenly furious out of nowhere, as if she were catching emotion on the fly. "I've seen the worst."

T. J. took her hand, lacing his fingers through her fingers, almost casually, fraternally.

"I get upset about children," he said. "That's why I wanted this film done to honor Meridian, I suppose. In a way the town has been my parents."

The headlights of a car slid over the ceiling, down the wall, across T. J.'s face.

"I think someone's here," Helen said, and before she had a chance to get up David Jaspersen had come in the front door with a flashlight.

"Helen?" he called, the yellow circle from the flashlight skipping across the floor.

"I'm here," she said.

"God, what a night," David said. "The river's on the rise and trees are down all over town.

"I was wondering where you were, T. J. The beech is down in your front yard. I think it may have been the tree that took the telephone wires down in this part of town."

"I couldn't get up the hill tonight in a wheelchair."

"I guess you couldn't. It's a real mess," David said. "Do you want to spend the night at my place?" He moved through the darkness to the living room.

"I'll go home," T. J. said. "If I come with you, can I get into the house?"

"The tree fell away from the house," David said. "You won't have any trouble."

He walked, following the large circle of light, into the kitchen and then back.

"Is there going to be a flood?" Helen asked.

"It's a storm passing over on its way east," David said, "so I don't think so."

T. J. lifted himself back in the wheelchair.

"I'll come back another night and watch the film with you," he said to Helen.

"I hope so," Helen said, wishing they would stay, wishing at least T. J. would stay with his warm comfortable voice.

"Tomorrow is Beatrice Tallis's funeral," David said. "Prudential told you?"

"She didn't mention it," Helen said, feeling her way to the front door.

"At 10 A.M. The weather better clear." He stopped for a moment, adjusted his flashlight for T. J. to see his way across the living room. "I hope a lot of people come."

"Won't they?" Helen asked.

"People have been less neighborly since the film," David said.

She opened the front door.

Already the wind had abated, the rain thinned to a steady rhythm of pine needles falling from the sky, a hint of moon on the horizon.

"We should have electricity soon," David said, "but I'll check with you early in the morning." He put his hand on her arm awkwardly as if it were a gesture he felt he should make but was uncomfortable making. "Are you okay?"

"I'm fine," Helen said, standing in the door watching them in the small light move down the steps to David's car. "Don't worry," she added. But she was worried.

She had had attacks of nerves since she was young. Panic attacks, her mother called them—their cause elusive. She could be about her business in school or walking along a street with friends or in the market, no known perpetrator around, her body reacting to invisible danger, her mouth dry, her heart beating too quickly, her breath caught in her throat.

Once she had been eating strawberries at a summer lunch with relatives in Michigan when it happened. Once she'd been sitting in algebra class daydreaming of kissing Peter Samuels and once at the market making a small dinner for other residents at the University of Michigan. She had fled to the street, her basket of eggplant and zucchini and a leg of lamb left in the middle of the aisle. Once the unnamed fear abated, and sometimes that took awhile, she searched for the cause.

The appeal of science to Helen was the reliability of a reality.

"What you get is, by and large, what is," her human biology professor had said early on in the first semester. "So the trick is to see well."

Helen saw very well. Her eyes were instinctual and she loved the reassurance the study of science promised of a measurable reality.

But now, sitting in an alarming darkness in the sterilized house of the pale, long-armed Dr.

Richard Hazelton, her hands holding tight to one another to keep from shaking, reality was slippery and Helen wanted to go home, not to Ann Arbor, but home to her childhood, her early childhood, to the time before Emma Fielding died.

9.

The storm had weight and density, moving by the front windows of the house with the sound a crowd makes. Helen was curled in the large chair with a safe view, comforted by the company of weather.

The night felt like Mackinaw when she was a child—lonely like Mackinaw where the weather had ongoing conversations and the people whose daily lives were determined by it bore silent witness.

In Mackinaw, Helen and her mother lived in Mrs. Peaches's guesthouse, which in the gray-black Michigan winter was empty—only Mrs. Peaches and her aged mother and Labrador retriever. Allie Fielding's shop was closed in winter and she spent her days in a makeshift studio weaving tapestries to sell in the summer tourist months.

There was a powerful loneliness on the island, a sense of being cast adrift. Often Helen went to school in the dark, home in the evening in the dark. She took piano from Mrs. Peaches's sister and played sports and listened to music at the Barn, where the youth of Mackinaw spent the winter evenings. She wasn't popular with her peers in the conventional sense, not in the center of things, but she was of great interest to them, a subject of private conversations, considered a whimsical figure, as if she were by temperament an expression of the mercurial nature of Mackinaw's weather. But she was an outsider on an island which was by its geography already outside and her daily life felt more like a ballad about a life than the experience of the thing itself. She glided through her years in high school—not unhappy necessarily, but uprooted. When she thought of herself as a child, uprooted was the picture she saw in her mind—a straggly wildflower of a girl overturned, the roots dangling, exposed to the air.

There was a stultifying pattern to her days—school and sports and meals with Mrs. Peaches, stews all winter long, the same stew with beef and too many carrots, grainy potatoes. There were lovely conversations with her mother. Never serious conversations. Her mother refused discussions of personal matters, almost as though she had no interior life to speak of. But in her mother's studio with the smell of paints and lacquer and glue, her mother looking like a girl in blue jeans and a long shirt, her hair tied up in a bandanna, their talks were warm and promising, almost satisfactory. Allie Fielding liked to talk about science although she knew very little scientific. Her interests were color and texture. She kept things in the way a woman with a scientific turn of mind might do—butterflies, dried flowers, bits of cast-off nature, feathers—and over mint tea and cookies they'd talk about things. Allie Fielding liked things. They were personal to her.

"Now see the oval brown spots on the yellow wings of that sweet butterfly," her mother might say. "I love brown and yellow together, especially in winter," or "Feel the softness of this feather on your cheek. Smell the earth on it."

They didn't talk about Dr. Philip Fielding, who had left when Helen was seven, although Allie spoke to him without acrimony when he called for Helen on Sundays. They never talked about the time before Emma died when they lived in Ann Arbor and Dr. Fielding taught at the University of Michigan. They didn't mention Emma at all.

"Nobody talks in our family," Helen said to her father in her senior year of high school, visiting him in Santa Cruz.

"What would you like to talk about?" he asked.

"Anything," Helen said.

"I'm happy to speak to you about anything," her father had said in his self-protective, absent-minded way.

"I want to talk about Emma dying," she had said, hearing, as she was speaking, his sharp intake of breath.

"No," her father said, not cross about it, rather weary and professorial. "You know we don't talk about Emma."

"Why don't we?" Helen had asked.

"It's too difficult for your mother and me," he said. "Much too difficult."

"Maybe later?" Helen asked.

"I don't think so," her father said. "I don't think Emma's death is a subject for our family."

The unspeakable, and by her parents' insistent silence, Helen was accountable, not for Emma's actual death, perhaps, but for the absence of her life.

"Nothing that matters is ever a subject for our family," Helen had said.

She must have drifted off to sleep and she awoke suddenly when the lights in Dr. Hazelton's house flickered on. It was just before 2 A.M. by her watch. The wind had stopped roaring by the window and it was raining light as feathers against the pane. Gregory climbed down from the couch, stretched and followed Helen to the kitchen where she turned on the gas for tea. She had awakened weighted by a sense of trouble she couldn't define, as if something specific had happened and she had lost the memory of it.

She made a piece of toast with jam, sitting at the kitchen table, feeling peculiar, the victim of a kind of painless heart attack.

* * *

At Aunt Martha's they had picked raspberries in the back garden, not Aunt Martha's garden but one belonging to someone else of whom Helen was afraid. They'd pick the raspberries off their prickly bushes in white cotton gloves which had belonged to Aunt Martha when she was a girl and then, sitting in the white Adirondack chairs, they'd eat them from a cold glass bowl.

The person whose raspberries they had picked was a woman—Helen could hear her voice, as small as the point of a needle, and the woman had a slender face with short curly beige hair, pale white skin and somewhere a purple stripe.

"Why does Mrs. Whatever"—she had lost the last name—"why does Mrs. Whatever with the raspberry patch have a purple stripe across her face?" she had asked her Aunt Martha.

"It's a birthmark," Aunt Martha had told her. "Most everyone has a mark of some kind when they are born."

"I don't," Helen had said.

"But Emma has a tiny tulip on her thumb," her mother said.

They had looked at Emma's plump thumb, at the little red flower on top of it.

"I don't like Mrs. Whatever's birthmark," Helen had said.

"But if everyone had a purple stripe across his face, darling, then you would think it was lovely," her mother said. "You'd want to have one just like it."

"I don't think so," Helen had said.

Sometime later, that evening perhaps, Helen had taken the juice in the bottom of the raspberry bowl and with her finger had drawn a little red tulip on her thumb.

The wind had died and she went upstairs to change for bed. By morning she would be exhausted, she thought, and what if there were an emergency? She ought to sleep. She needed to sleep. She didn't want to change to her nightgown. Perhaps if she slept in her clothes, needing to be prepared as if she could hear an emergency on its way. She lay down on top of the comforter, turned off the lights, closed her eyes but she lay awake, her eyes open, staring into the darkness. And she knew by the irregular stiffness of her back, the tenseness in her belly, that she would be awake for the rest of the night.

At 5 A.M., a slip of dawn lightening the sky, she was wide awake. She got up, put a blanket around her shoulders and went downstairs, turning on the VCR, which was stopped at the clinic with the figure of Dr. Richard Hazelton and Prudential at the clinic.

She replayed Ann Durham walking down the street holding the hands of the two little girls with their backs to the camera. The scene moves across the street, along the backs of the houses which face College Street, their low fences lined with trash cans now loaded on a pickup truck by a young redheaded boy in a navy pea jacket who knows the people in the houses by their first names. He is called Gaven by the narrator and, as the camera leaves him, he has picked up a yellow striped kitten and put him inside the fence of one of the houses.

"They watch over one another's houses and children and kittens," the narrator is saying. "Everyone—Gaven, the chief of police, the reverend of First Methodist—feels himself responsible."

She fast-forwarded the tape to the clinic. Dr. Hazelton turns to face the camera, holding the file. He has a loose, languid body, a way of dangling as if he were hanging from his shoulders instead of standing on his feet, a gentle, limpid face, too soft for Helen's taste. But something about him is familiar, his face perhaps, but maybe it is his long, long arms. His elbows hang below his belt; extended, his arms must hang to his knees.

She knew him. Certainly she knew him. Or did she? Was it just that by a certain age anyone—his face blending with other faces, his arms and gait and voice—seems familiar, seems to be a part of a particular childhood. And he could be, likely is, a perfect stranger.

Before the sun came up on the beginning of a new day in Meridian, Helen was in the pull-down attic of Dr. Richard Hazelton's house with Gregory stretched out on his back beside her. The attic was small and peaked but there was a window and a light, and what she found when she climbed up the narrow stairs was organized in cardboard boxes neatly labeled—COLLEGE BOOKS, MEMORABILIA FROM COLLEGE, MEDICAL SCHOOL BOOKS, FATHER'S PAPERS, LETTERS AND PHOTOS: CHILDHOOD; PHOTOS: COLLEGE AND MEDICAL SCHOOL; PHOTOS AND MEMORABILIA: MERIDIAN.

Helen opened the box marked MERIDIAN. It was organized by the year, beginning in the year of Richard Hazelton's birth, four years before her own, so she could have known him, could have seen him on the street when she visited her Aunt Martha, a man with such long arms. There were pictures of a couple on the front porch of a house, a cottage really, the mother a pale wisp of a woman holding a small baby. "Mother, Father and me: age two months" written in light pencil on the back. Several photos taken the same day with a different perspective, so in some the baby is recognizable as a particular baby, baldish with an expression of indifference on his face, and others, taken at a distance so the perspective allows the inclusion not just of the cottage with the young couple and baby on the front steps but the cottages on either side. On one side, the cottage with its wide front porch, its trellis of wisteria, is certainly Aunt Martha's house. So this baby, this boy, lived next door. Perhaps she remembered him. Perhaps they played.

There were many photographs in bunches, fifteen, twenty on a particular day and then years passed before another set of photos. The father, smaller than his wife and portly, probably older, maybe a great deal older, had disappeared in the photos by the time the boy was five or six, so the pictures showed the mother, who began to wear her hair on top of her head in a small ball. Often there was a large black dog with floppy ears. Helen noticed that there were no candid shots although the pictures had been taken with an ordinary camera. They were posed, the mother with her arm on the son's shoulder, awkward in the gesture as if the pose had been assumed for the photographer and was unpracticed in daily life, Dr. Richard Hazelton at five or six holding a violin, a book, standing next to a much older woman with a bunch of yellow flowers. There was a whole set of pictures of a grave, or several graves, white slabs of stone evenly lined up with a little flower bed in front—and several closeups of one grave, a new one, the baskets of wilting gladiolus lying on their sides, a picture of a plaque on graceful metal gates: MERCY CEMETERY. There was a group of pictures in front of Meridian Elementary with Dr. Richard Hazelton standing on the front steps, no children anywhere around, just the doctor as a boy, his long arms, long even then, hanging at his side. Stuck in between the files, Helen found an envelope marked MERIDIAN SUMMERS (Boyhood of R. Hazelton) and in the envelope were single pictures from different times—several photographs of the town, of Main Street and the house next to Aunt Martha's, some closeups, quite fuzzy, of a rose garden, of the Methodist church with a man who must have been the minister standing on the steps of the church with Dr. Richard Hazelton at maybe two or three.

She almost slipped by the picture of her own memory since the color in it had dimmed and the picture was a little rumpled but it was a picture of three children and a dog in front of the small cottage covered with climbing yellow roses and wisteria where Aunt Martha lived. The children stood in a line, posed for a photograph, first the boy, Dr. Richard Hazelton, perhaps six or seven years old with a new haircut so his pale face had a ghoulish aspect in the picture, then the dog, a black long-haired dog with a pointy nose, then Helen in white shorts and a T-shirt with writing on it which was illegible, then Emma, holding Helen's hand and with the other hand dragging an upside-down doll with long red hair.

Helen remembered.

Richie, next door to Aunt Martha, the son of Mrs. Whatever with the purple stripe—you couldn't see the stripe in the pictures. She leaned against the attic wall.

By morning she would try her mother once more and perhaps with any luck she could reach her. She was having trouble breathing again.

She lay down on the floor of the attic, waiting for dawn, her eyes closed, concentrating on absence, hoping to breathe.

She had come to Meridian by choice but the

consequence of memory restored was like weather, happening beyond her, out of sight but traveling in her direction.

10.

Wednesday was surprisingly beautiful after the long night storm. The sun was bright, the air clear although the weather report from Toledo promised a heat wave. The streets were almost completely dry. Families leaving First Methodist Church after the service for Beatrice Tallis talked about the river, how lucky they were to have avoided another flood bringing the possibility of more sickness.

Helen didn't go to the cemetery.

"You go. I'll be in the clinic," she said to Prudential, not wishing to be a stranger in attendance. "You've been here for years and know the family."

"Eleven years in September," Prudential said. "I'm thinking of going home to South Carolina."

"Not before the end of the summer, I hope," Helen said. "Not before I leave."

"Who knows?" Prudential said. "I don't plan far ahead."

They stood apart from the people spilling out of the church, shaking hands with the Tallis family, who had gathered at the top of the steps with Reverend Winters, a formality about the scene surprising in so small and isolated a town, Helen thought.

"I suppose you notice the ill will," Prudential said in a whisper.

"Ill will?" She looked over at Prudential. "Toward me?"

"I notice ill will," Prudential said.

"Is it from someone specific?" Helen asked.

"Who knows? People here expect a kind of miracle and you're just a physician," Prudential said, "nothing more." And then she did the oddest thing, right in front of everyone. She slipped her arm through Helen's in an open gesture of friendship, an act of taking sides.

"I have a nose for bad news," Prudential said. "It's in my genes."

They parted then, Prudential disappearing in the crowd of mourners gathering to walk to the cemetery.

Helen settled in at her desk with the charts. Of course the people in Meridian were suspicious. They were having a terrible time. It wasn't personal. She had to remind herself of that.

She changed the calendar, May 24, and taking the picture of Dr. Hazelton with her and Emma out of her pocket, she looked at it in the full light of day. It must have been taken the summer Emma died. Helen was four, fierce by the look of her picture, and Emma, an angel, had been two. The boy, Dr. Richard Hazelton, had an expression of indifference, no pleasure in the moment. Perhaps he had been required to spend time with the Fielding girls or was shy or sullen or bad-tempered. He had fish eyes—like Oliver, pale wet fish eyes, or so it seemed. His arms, which hung down straight on either side, had an unnatural look, rubber arms pulled to the full length of their potential. But it was the pale aspect of his face which tugged at the back of Helen's memory.

Now that the emergency with legionella was passing, the report of confirmation in from the lab, she needed to go to the hospital in Harrisville to see the patients from Meridian. There had been three of them in the hospital when she arrived. She read the charts. Charles Martel, age fifty-nine, had Dressler's syndrome after a heart attack, a not uncommon reaction of the nervous system to a damaged heart. Karen Read had been hospitalized with acute respiratory distress on Sunday as a result of asthma and Mary Baker had given birth to a premature baby by caesarean section, a boy born at twenty-six weeks, 2 lbs. 5 ozs., with mild respiratory problems. Helen called the attending doctor in Harrisville, Dr. Bartoli, an older man with a careful hesitation in his speech, a slight accent. Mr. Martel had fever and fluid in his lungs, swelling in the sac around his heart, both symptoms of Dressler's syndrome. Karen Read would be released that morning and the

Baker infant had been removed from a respirator and was breathing on his own.

Helen loved medicine. She loved the feeling of measurable accomplishment at the end of a day. She had a temperament for emergencies. She needed them, sought them out. Otherwise, there was no definition to her life, no real sense of a life at all. And she had a love affair with the scientific names of things. Mallolus. Malleus. Ossicles. Incers. She repeated them over and over in her head as if she were memorizing for an oral exam—and they seemed like poetry, the way they sounded on her tongue, their precision and clarity.

When she finished speaking with Dr. Bartoli, she called her mother, flushed with the usual anxiety of dialing her mother's number.

If she needed her mother, if she were ill or in distress, Allie Fielding would not come—would not be able to come. Her father would be there, at a remove, there in body, better than nothing. Which was as much as she could expect. It was clear to Helen that her mother's capacity for sustaining others was in permanent retirement.

The answering machine was on again. This time when she left a message her stepfather picked up. He was a lawyer, younger than her mother and quick-witted, maybe even kind, she wasn't sure. But there was something inauthentic about him which put her off and she had never got over the sense that he simply came to Mackinaw on vacation and stole her mother for good.

"Sleeping? At noon?" Helen asked. "Is she ill?"

"No." Her stepfather hesitated.

"Is she avoiding me?" Helen asked crossly.

"She'll call," he said. "Does she have your number?"

"I left it on the machine," Helen said but she gave it to him again.

Her father was chatty and cheerful.

"Hello, hello, my angel," he said when he answered the phone. "And how is the weather in the dreary Middle West?" He was only interested in the weather in Meridian, not in the town itself nor in Helen's return there. He hadn't seen the film. He didn't remember David Jaspersen or people named Jaspersen at all or the neighbors next door to Aunt Martha called Hazelton.

"We only spent two weeks with Aunt Martha," he said. "We didn't make friends."

He said Allie was not ill but fragile. She had been fragile when he met her as a young girl. Life, he said, had a way of dealing unequally with people. And she never liked to talk on the telephone.

"She got the short end of the stick," he said. "Or the long end. I can't remember which is which."

"Did we have a funeral for Emma?" Helen asked when the conversation was almost over and her father's mind was drifting to the particulars of eighteenth-century European warfare as it tended to do.

"We had a memorial service," he said.

"Where was it? I have no recollection at all."

"Ann Arbor," her father said.

"And was I there?" Helen asked.

"I don't remember. It was a difficult time," he said, changing the subject to a friend's son who had been diagnosed with something called Addison's disease and did she know of any treatments.

Prudential came back shortly after one o'clock just as the clinic was filling for afternoon hours.

"I don't like what's going on," she said to Helen, beckoning for Paula Weller sitting in the waiting room with her daughter Lisa. "Two months ago you wouldn't have a funeral in Meridian without everybody there. And today half the town stayed home and it's not only because of this epidemic."

She turned to Mrs. Weller. "Lisa has a fever?"

"I think she caught the sickness from Maria," Mrs. Weller said.

Prudential took Lisa in her arms and headed to the examining room. "Follow me," she said to Mrs. Weller.

"Before you go back, who do we have today?" Helen asked.

"We have Maria today," Prudential said. "Ann Durham called in about her younger child, Casey. She thinks he's caught it from Sallie."

Helen shook her head.

"It's not possible," she said, washing her hands. "You can't catch legionella from other people."

Prudential raised her eyebrows.

"Anyone else?" Helen asked.

Prudential checked her list. "We have Kathy Bauer with a bellyache, Sandy Case with a high fever, Mrs. Lennon has found a lump in her breast," she said. "And Madeleine Sailor."

Helen nodded. "Is Madeleine ill?"

"Not in body," Prudential said, and led the way down the corridor to the examining room.

Paula Weller sat in the examining room with Lisa on her lap. She was a small, pretty, frightened woman, defended by quick conversation, small talk which went on and on.

"I give her vitamins, three a day, even though she throws them up," she said, and "My mother lost her hair before she was fifty," and "I wish we got better fruit in the markets here. In New York City the fruit is wonderful and they don't even have trees." Lisa sat quietly on the examining table, her hands folded in her lap. "It's the sickness, isn't it?" Paula Weller asked finally.

"Has she had diarrhea?"

"No," she said. "But she threw up her vitamins this morning."

"What hurts?" Helen asked Lisa.

"Everything," the little girl said.

"Your arms?" She laid her cool hand against the child's cheek.

Lisa nodded.

"Does she have a dry cough?"

"Well, she has a cough but I don't know if it's wet or dry. My uncle got TB when he went to Russia, you know. There's lots of TB in Russia. It's epidemic."

"This isn't TB," Helen said.

"This is the sickness, isn't it?"

"I think it probably is. I'm going to treat her with erythromycin as if she has legionella although her fever isn't at all high."

Paula dropped her head in her hands. "I was afraid of this."

"It's good you got her here today. We've caught it very early," Helen said gently, touching the mother's shoulder. "She's going to be fine."

"I hope," Paula Weller said, holding Lisa, standing in the door ready to leave. "I didn't go to Beatrice Tallis's funeral today because I don't feel friendly toward people like I used to feel and I don't know why." She shifted Lisa to her other arm. "Now I feel bad. Bea Tallis was in Lisa's grade."

"You have a nice way," Prudential said when the Wellers had left. "I like doctors with a nice way."

Kathy Bauer was a tall slender nervous woman, about thirty, with a terrible stomachache. Prudential helped her into the examining room and by the time she was on her back in stirrups for a pelvic examination she was moaning out loud.

"It's not like a stomach flu," she said to Helen. "It's like nothing I've ever had before."

Prudential held her hand.

"It may be a cyst on the ovary," Helen said, examining her.

"Cancer? My mother died of cancer."

"Not cancer," Helen said, helping her lift her legs down. "I'd be surprised if it were more than a cyst."

"Pancreatic cancer. That's what she died of."

"What kind of equipment do they have in Harrisville, Prudential?" Helen asked. "Sonograms? CAT scans?"

"You have to go to Toledo for CAT scans," Prudential said.

Helen called the hospital in Toledo and sent Kathy Bauer in for tests.

Sandy Case had legionella.

"I'm pretty sure," Helen said, giving her a bag of samples of erythromycin and writing her a prescription.

"But I thought it only happened to children," she said. "I'm twenty-six."

"It happens to anyone," Helen said. "Children just seem to have been the ones susceptible in Meridian."

"I know who I caught it from," Sandy said. "I took care of Sallie last week while Ann went to Toledo."

"The doctor says this isn't the kind of disease

you catch from people," Prudential said skeptically.

"How do you know?" Sandy asked. "Everybody is getting it."

Helen sat down on a stool, across from her. "What we know about this illness is its symptoms, which are fever and chills, muscle aches, sometimes diarrhea and sometimes a dry cough and pleurisy," she said. "We know it can come from contaminated air cooling systems, which you don't have in Meridian, and from organisms in water."

Helen noticed a look pass between Prudential and Sandy Case but she went on. "We also know, because we have no evidence otherwise, it isn't passed through the air from person to person."

Sandy shrugged. "Maybe not other places," she said, gathering up her medicine.

"In Meridian, we make each other sick," Prudential said.

"You need to go to bed," Helen said, letting the remark go by. "Be sure to boil your water, drink lots of fluids and I'll drop by your house to check on you this evening."

"Mrs. Lennon tells me the lump she found in the shower this morning has disappeared," Prudential said. "So she went home."

Helen pulled off the paper on the examining table, cleaned the counter, dropped the disposable material in the trash can. "Prudential?" She folded her arms across her chest. "I have the sense that you doubt what I say about legionella."

"I doubt what everyone says," Prudential replied with a look of impenetrable calm.

"People asked me to this town because you needed a doctor," Helen said wearily. "If you have all the answers, I should leave."

"Suit yourself," Prudential said.

In her office, Helen opened the window and turned on the fan. It was almost five o'clock, hot and hazy, uncomfortably still. She took off her white starched jacket and unbuttoned her blouse.

When Prudential knocked, she was still sitting in her chair, her feet on the windowsill, half sleeping in exhaustion, but she jumped up with a start.

"Trouble," Prudential said.

"Trouble?"

"Madeleine Sailor is still here." Prudential stepped just inside the door and shut it behind her. "I told her we have house calls to make and she says she only wants a minute of your time."

"Okay," Helen said, buttoning her blouse, putting on her white jacket. "Send her in."

Madeleine Sailor seemed to be drunk. She was wearing a long pale peach silk skirt, a dressy skirt for evenings, and a sweater in the sweltering heat. On her chin she had a small red circle of lipstick exactly the size of the end of a lipstick tube. She sat down in the chair across from Helen, smiling a little cockeyed child's smile.

"You're looking at my beauty mark?" She touched the red circle with her finger. "It's really only lipstick but I'm calling it a beauty mark."

"Are you ill?" Helen asked, standing up, walking around her desk and leaning against it so she was looking down at Madeleine Sailor.

"Oh no, not ill at all," she said. "I'm perfectly fine. Perfectly fine fine fine. Do you remember that song? I used to sing it to Maggie. I'm perfectly fine fine fine," she sang, "all the time time time. Except when I'm blue." She laughed. "No. I came to see you not because I'm sick at all but with a message to you." She opened up her crocheted bag and took out a piece of paper which she unfolded carefully and handed to Helen. "That is my message."

Helen took the note. It was written on white typing paper with red Magic Marker. She read it and handed it back to Madeleine.

WATCH OUT, it said.

"Is that all?"

"That's all," Madeleine said. "I wrote it for you."

"Thank you very much."

"But it's a warning, don't you understand?"

"I do understand."

"I thought you should know there are people in Meridian who are not pleased to have you here."

"Are you one of them?" Helen asked.

"Oh no," Madeleine said. "I'm a friend."

"Then thank you for warning me." She helped

Madeleine Sailor out of her chair, walking her to the door, and in such close proximity she could smell the strong odor of alcohol on her breath.

"Have you seen the film yet?" Madeleine asked.

"Some of it," Helen said. "I'll see the rest this weekend."

"Call me if you have any clues," Madeleine said. "I'll be eternally grateful. Eternally. Eternally."

Helen stood at the door and watched her walk unsteadily up the street.

"Drunk?" Prudential asked.

"I think," Helen said.

"I'll call her husband to pick her up," Prudential said. "That's new. I don't think Madeleine ever had anything stronger than lemonade to drink."

"Poor woman. It's too awful for her." Helen packed her bag for house calls. "Where first?" she asked.

"We should go to the Durhams' and the Wellers'," Prudential said.

"What about Maria? Have you spoken to the Walkers?" Helen asked.

"Maria's almost herself again."

"And Sandy Case?" Helen said.

"She lives at the other end of town, beyond the rail station. We'll go there last."

"Have you heard from the hospital in Toledo about Kathy Bauer?"

"It was an ovarian cyst. They're keeping her overnight and want you to call."

Helen telephoned the hospital in Toledo, filled a thermos with ice water and headed out.

"Reverend Winters called to say you can use his car any time you need to go to the hospital."

"I'm going there tonight."

"He'll drive you there so you can find your way the first time."

It was the kind of hot day in which the air takes on weight, a pale yellow haze like a gauze curtain separates the eye from objects in the distance. Helen felt not ill exactly but unlike herself, unfamiliar in her head.

They moved along Main Street without conversation. Helen could tell that Prudential wanted to speak but she wasn't going to make it easy for her.

She opened the thermos.

"Water?" She handed it to Prudential. Then she dipped her fingers in and wiped her forehead. "Ungodly hot."

Prudential had fallen in step.

"You've walked into a hornets' nest," Prudential said finally.

"So it seems," Helen said.

"You're a nice woman and I like women a little edgy." She cocked her handsome head and smiled at Helen. "I'm sorry it's the way it is."

Helen laughed. "What way is it?" she asked, knowing the question wouldn't be answered.

They walked up the steep hill to the Durhams'

past Mrs. Barrett feeding her tabby cat on the front porch and Mr. Terry in a large straw hat tending his garden.

"A hornets' nest is fine for hornets as long as you don't walk into it," Prudential said. This seemed to please her. She wiped her damp hands on her cotton shirt, laughing a little to herself.

It was late when Helen got back from the hospital in Harrisville and only slightly cooler.

Ben Winters drove her home. He was a careful driver, apologizing if he made a small mistake, stopping the car too quickly, inching too far in front of a stop sign.

"You don't need to take me all the way home," Helen said. "Stop at your house. It's a nice night and I'd like to walk."

Ben Winters protested, full of good will—"Oh, let me take you, anything could happen."

"Like what?" Helen asked. "In Meridian?"

He laughed. "Of course not. Nothing happens in Meridian," he said. "But it's so dark out tonight, you can't even see the moon."

"I'll be fine," she said.

She walked along the silent, empty Main Street, hearing the river's distant locomotive roar.

The house was dark, a blue-gray darkness of early evening, but even before she walked in the front door she had an overwhelming sense that either someone was there or had been there moments before. She stood in the hall at the arch that led to the living room and turned on the light. On the white wall above a slate-gray couch and beside a large photograph from the turn of the century of Meridian railway station, written in black glossy paint in a large and messy scrawl, was

DR. HELEN FIELDING GO HOME.

And underneath HOME was a funny mark, a kind of frenzied animal with broad brush strokes, a porcupine perhaps, more troubling than the message.

IV.
Weather Report

The Story of
Merdian

Wednesday, April 11

The third day of the shoot of "Meridian," a bleak windy April Wednesday, difficult for filming, Peter Forester woke up early with a strange, unfamiliar euphoria, a kind of pleasant drunkenness, on a day whose weather would generally have put him on the edge of temper. He checked his watch—six-ten—got up, dressed, ran his fingers through his long thick hair and left quietly by the back door of the church hall.

The air was damp and cold to the bone so he walked quickly down Main, lit by a line of streetlights, pale yellow circles in the foggy dawn.

Sophie lived on Poplar Street, a long narrow street, straight uphill into the small forest that topped the cone of hills around Meridian. She had a small peach house with white shutters and, as he approached the bottom of Poplar, he was pleased to see a light on the second floor of her house. So she was up too, unable to sleep, thinking about him.

This hadn't happened to him before. He wasn't easily won over, known in his personal and professional life as focused and unflappable, subtle in his energy with unused pockets in reserve. He had been married once briefly and there was always a woman, generally tall and blonde, cool-tempered, witty, intelligent, deceptively fragile. He was predictable that way, predictable too in the excellence of his documentary films, known for his ability to make clear and moving the personal and humane in the flat linear format of documentary. Now suddenly he had this exhilarated sense of slipping.

He had looked at the clips the night before. Sophie, here and there—at the market, in the coffee shop, at the pharmacy, on the front steps of her house with Molly.

"This is absurd," T. J. Wisely had said to him. "If anyone in Meridian saw what I'm seeing, they'd ask us to leave town. Sophie isn't Meridian. She didn't come until a few years ago."

"I take your point," Peter Forester had said. "Don't worry your pretty head. I'm going to be able to make this story work."

But he couldn't help himself. He saw Sophie DeLaurentis as a fallen doe. He wanted to possess her, assume her, as if such union would somehow purify his heart. It wasn't physical or simply physical. But on the third morning of the Meridian shoot Peter Forester's destination was sex.

The telephone rang in the dark but Sophie was already up, propped in her bed, thinking about what to wear for tomorrow's shoot and should she change her hair style. Maybe "up" would be pretty. They had told her to wear makeup, especially with her dark skin. Red, red lips were striking, they said, although ordinarily she didn't wear any color. She turned on the light next to her bed.

"Hello," she said quietly, so as not to wake Molly sleeping at the end of the hall.

"Sophie," Dr. Richard Hazelton said.

"It's too early," Sophie said. "I'm still sleeping."

"I want Molly out of this film," he said. "I spoke to Ann Durham yesterday afternoon and you're making Molly into a little starlet. She's just a baby."

"I'm not doing anything," Sophie said. "The film crew makes the decision."

"I'm coming over today before my office hours to pick her up," Richard Hazelton said. "She can play in the waiting room. Prudential will keep an eye on her."

"Not today, Richard, please," Sophie said. "They're doing play group today and then they're doing your office. They told me I was to bring her to your office with a sore throat."

He hesitated. "Does she have a sore throat?"

"She could have. I mean we're supposed to pretend she has a sore throat. The film needs a story line, Peter says, and Molly and I are sort of it," Sophie said. "Besides, today is Mona Dickenson's viewing. They'll be doing the viewing and I'm not taking Molly there."

"I'm certainly glad to hear that," Richard said.

"I'll be over for coffee and we can talk about it then."

"Maybe tomorrow, Rich," Sophie said, "we can have coffee tomorrow." But he had hung up.

Downstairs, she heard what sounded like a knock on the front door. She went to the head of the stairs and looked down. There in the paned window at the top of the door she could see the thick black curly hair of Peter Forester.

She ran to the bathroom, opened the window and called, "I'll be right down in just a second."

David Jaspersen was just making coffee when Richard Hazelton knocked on the front door.

"Trouble?" David asked, leading him into the kitchen. "It's not even seven o'clock yet."

"No trouble," Richard Hazelton said. "No one is sick."

Richie Hazelton had been a strange boy growing up in Meridian, just odd enough with his long arms, his troubling self-consciousness, to be worrisome to people his own age. There was something disturbing about him. In high school he had been ridiculed but his peers were cautious, sensing him capable of unpredictable behavior.

As an adult, he was quiet, without the capacity for small talk, and David assumed he had acquaintances but few friends. This morning, however, David was aware of something different in Rich Hazelton. He sat across from David at the kitchen table in his white physician's coat and tie, thin-lipped, pale, trembling just beneath the skin, a subcutaneous muscle revolution.

"I don't want Molly in the film," he said.

"None of us ought to be in the film," David said. "But there isn't much we can do about it."

They had coffee. David made toast and offered Dr. Hazelton cereal which he refused. Upstairs he could hear Win getting out of bed for school.

"Most everyone in town is pleased this is happening, as I'm sure you know," David said.

"I know," Dr. Hazelton said.

"I don't like it because it's too complicated to have these extra people around." David poured them another cup of coffee. "And I don't like it because people are willing to do anything to get seen on television." David let the dog in the back door.

"That's it," Rich said, his face filling with color. "Like Sophie." He shook his head. "She's an idiot."

"I wouldn't expect anything else of her," David said.

"But Molly"—Rich Hazelton held his head with his hands—"children shouldn't have to be what their parents make them. If Sophie wants to—" He broke off mid-sentence. "Don't you think?" he asked David. "If Sophie wants to, that's her business but she shouldn't push Molly onto her stage."

David shrugged. "Parents have done that with their children for a long time."

"Well, it's very wrong," Rich said.

Win called and David went upstairs to check on him. When he came back down, Rich Hazelton was in the hall.

"Thanks," he said to David. "I suppose I just needed to blow off steam before I drop by Sophie's for coffee."

"No trouble," David said, and they shook hands.

He watched Dr. Hazelton walk down the steps, across the street, through the Angels' side yard, the shortcut to Sophie's, two blocks directly east of David's.

Then he picked up the telephone and dialed Sophie's number. She answered on the first ring.

"Can I call you back?" she asked in a soft curly voice.

David said not to bother. He had to go to work and would see her later, probably at Mona Dickenson's viewing.

"Do you happen to know the weather for today?" Sophie asked.

"Only what I see outside the window. Not a filmmaker's dream day," David said and hung up.

"So," David said when Win sat down to breakfast. "Has the film crew got many shots of you and your friends?"

Win shook his head. "They're supposed to do a baseball game. We were asked to dress up tomorrow to play on the high school field but they haven't got any pictures of me except maybe one looking at comics at the drugstore yesterday." He finished his cereal and put his bowl in the sink. "Danny O'Neill says the only kids they're filming are Molly DeLaurentis and Sallie Durham." He got his snow jacket, baseball cap, his book bag, kissed his father good-bye and left for school.

Dr. Richard Hazelton walked across the Angels' yard. Danny Angel, who worked in construction in Harrisville, was up and dressed in the kitchen and opened the window when Dr. Hazelton passed by.

"Trouble?" he called.

"No trouble," Rich replied. "I just had coffee with the chief of police and I'm headed through your yard to Poplar." He didn't mention Sophie by name.

"Have you been in the movie yet?" Danny asked.

"Not yet," Rich said.

"Me neither," Danny called and shut the window.

Richard Hazelton had grown up in Meridian, the last child of older parents, his father dead by the time he was six. For a long time, most of his childhood until he won the state science prize in ninth grade, his mother worried that he was too timid for the world, too strange, that he might in fact never have the emotional strength to leave home. All the way through school, even after the science prize, he was the object of ridicule especially from boys his own age. The only pleasant social time he had was with older ladies in the neighborhood. But the science prize, won for an experiment in chemical properties of weather, focused his floating energy, slipped him onto a track from which he never deviated until he met Sophie DeLaurentis.

He was seventeen when he went to college, twenty-two when he graduated from medical school at the top of his class and twenty-five when he received a Ph.D. in molecular biology. He was offered jobs everywhere, in labs, in teaching, as a scientist at large universities, but what he wanted in his heart and soul was to return to Meridian to his small town where the only doctor was a family doctor, in charge of the health of all of the citizens of the community. He wanted to matter to the people from his lonely childhood.

He was happy in Meridian. People were kind to him, depended on him, invited him to dinner and cookouts and family reunions. He had what passed for genuine friends, which he had never had before. He had his own house, which he organized the way his laboratory had been organized at Michigan, and a straight-spoken nurse in Prudential, who treated him with dignity. He was a part of a life which as a young man growing up had seemed unlikely to ever happen.

When Sophie DeLaurentis stayed the night at his small clapboard house early in November just before his thirtieth birthday, he was still a virgin.

He had never kissed a woman or held her hand or even been alone with one younger than sixty except professionally. He had thought about Sophie. She was the kind of luscious woman men did think about but he had never expected she would take an interest in him.

And it happened so fast, he could hardly catch his breath. One afternoon she came into the clinic with a fever and by that evening she was lying on top of the sheets of his bed, a soft golden body with large perfect breasts and a mass of black curly hair against his pillow.

At the time, she was married to Mr. DeLaurentis and before the year was out she would be a widow. For weeks afterward, she came to Rich Hazelton's house in secret. She never told him that she loved him or made promises although he spilled out his own declarations of love. But he knew she loved him, must love him, or why else would she come to his bed?

During those months, almost seven of them from the beginning of November until June, two months before Molly was born, they were together. It was almost impossible for Dr. Hazelton to maintain his practice of medicine with the internal explosion of his heart.

He felt as if he flew everywhere, a heavy bird flying low over the branches like an oversize sparkler scattering light.

Sophie never said it was his child. But how not? he asked himself. Certainly the child didn't belong to Mr. DeLaurentis at fifty-nine with a bad heart.

He planned to marry her later, maybe August, after the baby was born and the year of mourning nearly done. And they'd move, maybe to the old Duncan place just north of town with more land and a larger house.

Meanwhile, she came less and less often to visit him. First it was once or twice a week and then once in two weeks. He assumed that was the pregnancy. He was worried but he was too much of an innocent with women to prepare himself for her announcement that the affair was over.

"I planned to marry you," he said. "To raise our child."

"But, Rich," Sophie said, "the baby is Antonio DeLaurentis's baby."

"That's not possible," Richard said. "I'm a doctor. I know it. It's not possible."

She shook her head. "You don't know everything."

She broke his heart.

When Molly was born on the first of August, Richard Hazelton knew. She was his child, his small unclaimed treasure from the love affair of his life—the long almond-shaped eyes, the narrow head and slender fingers; the hair was Sophie's and the coloring and the full lips. But she was his daughter and though Sophie never once agreed that it was a possibility—"I was pregnant before I slept with you," she said—Richard

Hazelton laid claim and all the bits and shreds of his shattered heart belonged to that baby.

He walked around the back of the Angels', through the Beeches' yard, across the Durhams' garden and then to Sophie's. Sophie's house was small and the garden fenced to keep wildlife out of the vegetables in summer but as he came up to the side of the house beside the kitchen, looking in the window, what he saw was Sophie leaning against the fridge kissing the tall, slender director from CBS television.

Mona Dickenson's viewing was at home, her mother's house, a white clapboard set back from Main Street on Snow's Court.

David Jaspersen went early although the hours weren't set until afternoon. He wanted to talk to Mona's father about the filming. According to T. J., the family had approved.

But when he walked through the high white gate, T. J. was already there talking to Tommy, Mona's young husband, and her mother.

"The casket's open," Mona's mother said. "She went so quickly, the cancer didn't have a chance to eat her up like it did her father, so she looks just as lovely as she always did."

"She was a beauty," David said, kissing Mona's mother. "The one true beauty we've sent out from Meridian."

"I was talking to Tommy about the film crew," T. J. said to David.

"You're sure you want this to happen today?" David asked Tommy Dickenson.

"I don't mind but I don't want them inside the house." Tommy leaned against the fence, too weary with sadness to stand. "But if the film people are outside—quietly, quietly—I don't want a circus, T. J."

"You don't have to have anything, Tommy," T. J. said.

Tommy shook his head. "That guy, Peter, the director—stopped by last night. He made it seem all right. He said he'd heard from everywhere that Mona was beautiful," and he excused himself with a small complicitous wave to David and T. J. so he didn't break down in their company.

David shook his head. "I can't believe the invasion of privacy."

"Peter Forester's character is not my responsibility," T. J. said, wheeling along the road toward the Catholic church, lit from above by an early morning sun threatening to make a full appearance.

"I'm not holding you accountable for everything, T. J.," David said.

"You're a prince," T. J. said.

The day had turned when the viewing started at three—a clear spring day with a full distant sun, a deep blue sky; the colors of Meridian were spectacular. It was cold, not a harsh cold, so the front door of the house was open, Tommy and Mona's mother, her sister Nora, Tommy's parents, greeting people as they arrived, and the line formed quickly at three. By three-fifteen it was all the way down Snow's Court to Main Street.

The film crew was in the front garden, set up well beyond the assembly, and there was an almost crazy explosive excitement among them.

"It's like a circus," David said to Sophie, coming up behind her in the line of mourners.

She had come alone. The camera had actually followed her from Main Street, up Snow's Court, an angle from the side as she rushed up the street, with tiny steps, constricted by her long straight black skirt, her high, high heels. She had on a white-collared blouse, a long black coat and a brightly colored silk scarf, reds and oranges and yellows.

"Peter said the black and white didn't show too well on color film so he gave me this scarf," she told David when he asked why such a splash of color at a wake.

He wanted to hit her. He actually could feel the clear and urgent sense of picking her up and throwing her down Snow's Court to Main.

Peter Forester, dressed for the occasion, moved in on the crowd, picking up bits of conversation, zooming in on the faces of the community. There was even a still shot of a picture of Mona which Madeleine Sailor had—a lovely black and white head shot from her senior yearbook.

"I remember her when she was very young," Mr. Rubin was saying to Danny O'Connor and his wife. "She looked like an angel then and she looks like an angel now." He shook his head. "I haven't wept to do anyone for years. But when her body came to the funeral parlor yesterday morning, I wept."

"Did she look bad?" Mrs. O'Connor asked.

"She looked beautiful," Mr. Rubin said. "Liver cancer can be fast and merciful and hers was."

On the outskirts of the group of mourners, Mona's golden retriever stood, a black satin ribbon around his neck, a white rose stuck in the tie, and Peter Forester focused on the dog, who cocked his head.

Peter walked to the front of the line where a grim Madeleine Sailor stood with Henry and their daughter Maggie.

"She was in your class, wasn't she, Madeleine?"

Madeleine nodded. "I loved her," she said, restrained, her voice thin. "She was my closest friend and Maggie's godmother."

"It was so fast."

Madeleine nodded. "We were always known as the goody girls in class," she said softly. "But no one knew what really went on with us, how we smoked just there in the barn behind Mona's house"—she folded her hands under her chin demurely—"and drank very bad Gallo wine and, once when we were only fourteen, T. J. found us swimming naked in the river and stole our clothes." She smiled. "We had to run home with nothing on."

"They were a perfect couple," Mrs. Rubin said when David Jaspersen came up behind her. "What children they could have had, right, David? And Tommy Dickenson's the only one but you we thought was going to amount to something beyond Meridian."

"He already has," David said, moving back in the line to Sophie, who stood quiet and prayerful, conscious of the camera on her right, scanning her each time she focused on the conversation of a group of mourners.

"Where's Molly?"

"Dr. Hazelton has her in the clinic today," Sophie said. "Prudential is probably looking after her. I didn't want her here of course."

"Maggie Sailor is here and Sallie Durham," David said.

"But their mothers knew Mona. I never did. She had already left for college before I married Mr. DeLaurentis and moved here." She smiled. "Remember?"

T. J. Wisely was in the corner of the garden, his jaw fixed, his arms wrapped tight across his chest.

"Having a blast, T. J.?" David asked.

"Knock it off, David."

"At least your friends from Hollywood aren't disruptive."

"No, but if you pay attention, you'll discover they have about forty shots of Sophie and the rest of the dog."

"I'm sorry, T. J.," David said. "But they're

trying to make the most of this dramatic opportunity, right?"

"Shut up."

"How do you get the feeling without inventing the fact?" David asked, leaning against T. J.'s wheelchair. "This film is about feeling, right?"

"This film is important to me," T. J. said quietly, pulling his wheelchair over to a clump of trees. "It means everything. Meridian was my parents."

In the final shot of the finished film after the garden was empty of people, the front door of the Dickensons' house closed, dusk settling, Peter Forester had a frame of the long french doors lined with thin lace curtains in the front of the house, the outline of Mona Dickenson's casket in the background, and in the foreground her golden retriever lay on the front step, the white rose, its petals sheared, beside him.

11.

Helen stood in the window watching for David Jaspersen.

It was almost midnight and when she called he had been sleeping.

"'DR. HELEN FIELDING GO HOME' is what it says," she told him.

"I'm so sorry," David said.

"The paint on the wall is still wet," she said. "Whoever did it must have finished just before I came home."

"I'll be right over."

She was too upset to search the house although she was sure the message had been written by someone who came in the house and left right away. A person wouldn't hide out and wait for her. If he had in mind to hurt her, why would he bother to write a message announcing himself? She thought of Madeleine Sailor with her warning but that poor drunken woman was not capable of the bold statement splashed on the white walls of Helen's house.

She picked up Gregory and pressed him against her. It was taking David Jaspersen too long and the earth seemed to be quaking around her. She had been in an earthquake once in San Francisco with her father in the middle of the afternoon in a restaurant high over the bay. It was not even a large quake but there was no announcement that the earth was about to shift, no warning, just a funny feeling under the floor where her feet were resting, a sense of being a little drunk, the room spinning, some customers spilling out of their chairs, rushing to an archway, and then it was over, not even a rumble, just a momentary alteration. But it felt dangerous to Helen, coming so quickly, just a whisper of danger, a reminder, and then it was gone.

"What was that?" Helen had asked her father.

"A tiny earthquake," her father said. "Wasn't that an earthquake?" He leaned over to the table next to them where a man and a woman were reading their menus. The woman looked up.

"I believe so but who can tell, it was so small."

"I want to go home," Helen said, getting up from the table.

"We're safer here," her father had said.

"I want to leave now," she'd said. "I don't like the earth to change without telling first."

She had grown up with weather, on a comma in the middle of Lake Michigan, buffeted by weather as it rushed up and down and across the United States, and she didn't like it. She wanted to be able to read the weather report in the newspaper and count on what it said. Tomorrow will be calm and sunny, below freezing with no change in sight. Even dependable rain was better than a question mark, the earth slipping underneath her feet as if the planet itself was malleable as a putty ball.

The air in Dr. Richard Hazelton's house was thinning and she leaned against the couch with Gregory, too lightheaded to watch at the window for David Jaspersen to come. The last she remembered, she was thinking she must sit down quickly.

She and Emma had a seesaw at Aunt Martha's—or maybe it was in the backyard of the house in Ann Arbor. She couldn't remember. After Emma died, her mother never returned to the house. They put it up for sale and her father packed the boxes. Helen did remember going with him into the house, which in her memory was very large with long windows opened in summer onto a field. Perhaps that's where the seesaw had been. She knew it was red, that Emma sat on one end and she on the other, but because she was so much heavier than Emma, she was not supposed to sit down with her full weight on the seesaw, keeping Emma up in the air where she might fall.

"Be careful of Emma," her mother would call from the upstairs window. "She might fall."

She did fall once. Helen couldn't remember the circumstances or what happened when she fell or if she was hurt or even cried. But she could see Emma in her mind's eye tumbling through the air as if she had fallen from a great height, tumbling over and over toward the ground.

Helen saw headlights, not headlights exactly, but lights moving through the trees toward where she was lying, and what she saw in the wide light from a high moon almost at full circle was Emma Fielding tumbling through the dark gray summer sky toward earth.

"I can't stop shaking," she said to David, who sat next to her on the couch where she was lying. "Was I unconscious?"

"You were lying on the floor and your eyes were open," he said.

She took her own pulse. "Rapid," she said.

Her mouth was dry and her breathing shallow. "I think I fainted," she said, taking hold of his hand. "A syncopal attack caused by fear." She smiled. "Syncopal has such a nice musical sound. Mmm." She closed her eyes. "I feel weird," she said. "This hasn't happened to me before." She tried to regulate her breathing, to put her mind another place but the all-over shaking wouldn't stop.

David had stood up and was checking the writing on the wall.

"I'm sorry," he said. "I'm truly sorry. Whoever did it was thorough. The paint's enamel."

She kept her eyes closed.

"I have an extra bedroom," he offered. "You can stay there tonight."

"Maybe I will." She sat up on her elbow, resting her head in her hand. "Who do you think could have done it?" she asked.

He shook his head. "I don't know."

"Madeleine Sailor?"

She told him about the warning Madeleine had written.

"It's not in her character," David said, standing back to look at the painted wall. "I've known Madeleine all my life."

Helen stood up slowly, holding onto the side of the couch.

"Something is really the matter in Meridian, isn't it?" she asked. "It's not just bacteria."

"Something seems to be." He put his arm around Helen's waist.

"I'm fine," she said, stepping away from him. "I'd just like to get out of this house before a time bomb goes off."

"There's no time bomb," David said, taking her hand, turning off the lights.

"Who knows?" she said, still lightheaded and a little sick.

"Who do you think wants me out?" Helen asked as they drove down Main Street in the soft darkness, all the houses still as dollhouses. "Everyone?"

"That's difficult to say. I don't know. There are a few people who could be having a hard time with a stranger getting to know people's personal histories, which you do since you're a doctor."

"But they wanted a doctor. You had to get a stranger."

"People aren't necessarily pleased to get what they want," he said, pulling to a stop in front of his house. He put his hand on her cheek.

Someone was in Helen's room. It was morning but very early, dawn maybe, and she could feel the presence of another person. Somewhere she heard conversation.

When she opened her eyes, a boy, maybe seven or eight, very blond with a square English haircut and lazy-lidded eyes, stood at the end of her bed.

"Hello," she said, sitting half up, still dressed in the clothes she had on the day before. "I'm Helen Fielding."

"I know," he said. "I saw you when you came on the train from Detroit."

"You must be David's son," she said.

"Are you his girlfriend?"

"No," she said. "I spent the night because there was a problem at my house."

"He told me." The boy made no effort to move. "Maybe he's found the person who messed up your house," he said. "She's downstairs talking to my father."

He sat down on the end of the bed.

"She's crying," he said with a certain pleasure.

"That's too bad." Helen threw off her covers and got up. "Who is she?"

"You know about Maggie?"

"Maggie?"

"Maggie Sailor. The girl who was stolen."

"I have heard about her," Helen said, brushing her hair with her fingers.

"That's her mother downstairs crying."

"And you think she's the person who wrote on the walls of my house?" She could hear a woman downstairs sobbing. "It doesn't seem like the kind of thing she would do."

Win shrugged. "We think a stranger stole Maggie, so Madeleine doesn't like strangers."

Helen went through her things and took out her toothbrush.

"The bathroom's across the hall," the boy said. "It's a little dirty and you can't turn on the cold water, so be careful."

"Could I borrow a brush?"

"I think we have one." Win looked through a dresser. "I don't have a mother, so things are pretty messy."

"Where is your mother?" Helen asked.

"I don't even know her except she has yellow hair like mine and freckles and, when she left us, she married the chief of police in Madison, Wisconsin, where we lived. That's why my father changed from being a lawyer to the chief of police." He lay down on the bed where Helen had been sleeping. "I'll wait till you come out of the bathroom."

In the bathroom Helen washed her face. She decided against the brush, which was thick with beige hair and grease, but she found some mouthwash and a tiny bar of soap, no toilet paper, and the water, as Win had warned her, only ran hot.

Madeleine Sailor sat at the kitchen table with her head in her arms and, when Helen came downstairs, David motioned her away, excused himself and followed her to the front door.

"You may have been right," he said. "It could have been her."

"You think?" Helen said.

"I don't know," he said, walking across the front porch with Helen, down the steps, along the brick walk to the street. "She called me this morning because someone in Grace, Ohio, claims to have seen Maggie. And just after she called, T. J. called to say he had seen her come out of your house last night."

"But it doesn't seem like a thing she would do, does it? That's what you said last night."

David shrugged. "Who knows?"

Helen checked her watch—seven thirty-five—pinned her hair back up. "Call me if you find out anything."

"I will," he said. "Are you better today?" David asked.

"I'm fine," Helen said.

She wasn't entirely fine. She felt a kind of weakness as if it were her first day up from the flu.

"I'll check in with you later to be sure you haven't died," David said.

"Sweet of you," she laughed. He didn't kiss her but she thought he was going to—it felt as if he wanted to kiss her.

"See you later." He waved. So did Win, who had come out on the front porch, waving and waving.

Prudential was already at the clinic when Helen arrived.

"I heard the news," she said.

Helen slipped into the chair next to her, out of breath after the short walk.

"It's not the town it used to be," Prudential said without looking up but there was genuine sympathy in her voice.

"Things change," Helen said, looking through the folders of patients.

Prudential shook her head. "Not by accident," she said, picking up the ringing telephone.

"Meridian Clinic," she said. "Bring her right over." She took out the Hart chart from the file. "Cinder Hart spilled hot water from the stove down the front of her." She hung up the phone. "Last month it was her finger in a light socket."

"Have there been a lot of calls?"

"Four on the machine when I came in—Sallie Durham is coming over during clinic hours, Billie Bliss, Mr. Rubin, the funeral director, has bronchitis and Penny Noels has a rash on her chest." Prudential cocked her head. "Why doesn't a woman like you have a boyfriend or a husband—old as you are and not bad-looking?"

"I tried that," Helen laughed.

"So have I," Prudential said cheerfully. "More than once."

"I don't know about husbands," Helen said, and for a moment before Mrs. Hart flew through the front door of the clinic with Cinder and her baby daughter, the two women were cheerful conspirators, actual friends, and Helen felt a breath of safety in a hostile camp. She moved her chair closer to Prudential on the pretext of checking a chart, moved her arm next to hers, grateful for the comfort of flesh. "I have a lot to know before I'm ready for a husband."

"It's probably not worth knowing," Prudential said.

Cinder was a blond, pale, silent child, burned on her right arm and her shoulder and her neck.

Mrs. Hart sat in a chair across the room, holding her baby. She shook her head.

"I don't know what's the matter with her," she said to Helen, who was bathing Cinder's burns in ice water. "Every time she touches anything, it's a disaster. She even rode her new bike into a tree and it's got training wheels."

Prudential leaned against the examining tables, took a deck of cards from her pocket and handed Cinder the queen of diamonds.

"You put that under your pillow tonight and don't move it," she said to Cinder as she clutched the playing card. "You know what that card is?"

"Queen," Cinder said.

"Queen of what?"

"Queen of diamonds."

"And if you put her under your pillow, you're going to stop having the accidents you've been having. You understand?"

Cinder nodded. "No more accidents," she said, kissing the plastic double face of the queen of diamonds.

Helen sat down on a stool, pulling it over to Mrs. Hart. "This looks like mostly first-degree burns which involve only the top layer of skin. Except here." Helen pointed to a line of burn from the shoulder to the wrist on Cinder's forearm. "This appears to be second-degree, which is the second layer of skin." She took the ointment Prudential had given her. "I'll dress the wounds with this ointment and you should give her plenty of juices. Not so much water."

"This all started in late April after the film people were here," Mrs. Hart said. "First Cinder just crossed the street in front of Tom Reem's car without looking, didn't you, sweetheart?"

Cinder closed her eyes.

"And then she was bitten by a dog who never bites. Remember, Prudential? The Mullinses' white dog."

She stood up and put her baby on her hip. "And then the bicycle."

Helen lifted Cinder to the ground. "These burns are painful," she said.

"She shouldn't have touched the boiling pot." Mrs. Hart buried her face in her baby's soft hair. "Have you seen the film?"

"A little of it," Helen said.

"Cinder was the lead in *Snow White* and they showed the play on the film. There's also a shot of her at the pharmacy with a lollipop and walking to school with Sallie Durham," she said. "It went to her head." She excused herself and went to the Ladies.

"Does it hurt when I touch it?" Helen asked Cinder quietly. Her eyes were still closed but when she opened them, Helen noticed how clear an blue they were—not a bright blue but clear, and she found herself moved by the pure color of such blue eyes. "Does it?" Helen asked again.

Cinder looked up at her and didn't flinch.

"I hate my baby sister," she said.

Emma was born in early October on a Sunday, wet and cold in Ann Arbor. Helen remembered the weather because her absent-minded father took her to the hospital without a raincoat and she sat in the waiting room with a nurse who took off her wet clothes and put her in a hospital gown while her father went to see her mother. When she first saw Emma, she was wearing that dreadful hospital gown and what would Emma possibly think of her looking so foolish? Her mother, in a wheelchair, held the baby over to her, saying, "Be careful." "Be careful of Emma" as if by touching her Helen would do harm.

DO NO HARM.

She and Emma were someplace dark and damp with the smell of mothballs—maybe an attic, maybe the attic of Aunt Martha's where the pictures of her father as a child were in boxes, where the dolls with china faces from Aunt Martha's childhood were lined up against the wall.

"Be careful of Emma," her mother called from somewhere far off.

Emma sat on the floor of the attic in her yellow sunsuit, holding an old baby doll in her chubby arms.

"Be careful of Emma in the attic," her father called.

Why should she be so careful of Emma? What could happen to a plump smiley little girl with a worrying mother and father? And what about Helen? She could fall out of the attic window, three stories down to the slate patio. She could catch on fire. That didn't seem to matter very much to them. She could die.

"I hate you," Helen said to the plump child, her sister, sitting happily at her feet.

"How bad was that burn?" Prudential asked after the clinic hours were over and Helen was leaving to meet David Jaspersen and go back to her house.

"Not bad," Helen said. "I made a fuss because the mother was being terrible to her child."

"People go bad like peaches," Prudential said. "They start to go bad one place and before you know it they're rotten through and through." She stuck a pencil behind her ear and checked through the appointments for the afternoon. "I'll stay here through lunch," she said.

David Jaspersen was already at Richard Hazelton's house when Helen got there, standing on the front porch with his large hands in his pockets directing the painters who were finishing the wall.

"Let it dry and then go over it," David said to the two young men. "Did you sand it first?"

They nodded.

"Has the writing disappeared?" Helen asked, coming up on the porch.

"Not exactly," David said. "Not yet."

The writing on the wall was dim but still clear enough to read through the paint.

"I don't know what to say." David leaned

against the porch railing. "You can stay with me until we can find you another place."

Helen shook her head. "It doesn't seem to matter where I stay," she said. "It's that I'm here at all."

He walked outside and leaned against the porch railing, an expression on his face as if he were about to speak but had changed his mind.

"You were going to say something?" Helen asked softly.

"What would you like to do?" he asked.

"I don't know. Go back to Ann Arbor before long, I suppose," she said. "There're too many secrets here."

David brushed an imaginary insect from her face.

"It's not that secrets are being kept from you in particular. It's that we don't trust strangers, we don't even seem to trust each other." He followed her down the steps. "Your mother called."

"My mother?" Helen asked.

"One of the painters told me."

"What did she say?"

"Just call back."

Helen went inside and picked up the phone.

"You're sure it was my mother?" she said to the painters.

"That's what she called herself," one of the painters said.

Helen dialed the number, her heart racing. She felt the way she used to feel after her father left, after they moved to Mackinaw, waiting on the steps of the island school for her mother to pick her up, her mother late, so often late, and Helen thinking, Will she come soon, will she come at all, has she left by boat for the mainland? Now she could see her mother from years of watching her sitting quietly at the window of her room in Mrs. Peaches's guesthouse, her slender legs drawn up under her chin, looking into the middle distance, hoping for a sign of good news.

It was the answering machine. "Please leave a message at the beep." But Helen did not.

"She also left a message on the machine when I was in the john," the painter said. "I heard her voice. So she called twice."

Helen played the messages.

"Helen, it's Allie." There was a little giggle. "Your mother, Alice Fielding. I have a bad feeling. Your father agrees. I spoke with him just a while ago. We think maybe you shouldn't be in Meridian. Please call."

Helen picked up the telephone again and dialed, waiting for the beep on the answering machine.

"Mama, you never answer my calls and I have to talk to you. I have to talk to you about Emma. Mama? Are you just sitting there listening to me?" She put the phone down and dialed her father, who answered on the first ring and out of breath.

"I have a question," she said, not allowing him

the opportunity to frame a careful response. "Do you and Mama blame me for what happened?"

"Of course not, Helen," her father said. "What happened was an accident."

"But I don't really believe in accidents," Helen said. "I see them all the time in the hospital and they're not accidents. They're carelessness."

"Well," her father began, and was he going to say yes, of course, that was true, it had been careless of Helen?

Whatever had gone on by the river when Emma disappeared had been careless, someone's carelessness, and since Helen had been the witness, it must have been, hers.

"It was my fault," she said. And the words, spoken like a confession, in the closed dampness of a confessional box, were sufficient for Helen to acknowledge a complicity with fate which had determined the course of her life.

12.

It was after six in the evening, not yet dusk, but the sun was sliding over the hills, lighting the sky a soft silver.

The wall in the living room of Dr. Hazelton's house had been painted linen white, coat after coat of paint, and the house smelled of it but Helen could still read the writing, although it wasn't actually visible. The imprint was permanent, whether the words were there or hidden by layers of linen white.

Now, although she knew the house was empty, had checked the closets and under the bed and even the pull-down attic stair, she felt uneasy as if there were always someone in the house just beyond her hearing.

When Emma died, her parents took down the pictures, all the ones of Emma alone and of the whole family and all but one of Emma and Helen, that taken from the back, the girls sitting side by side facing Lake Michigan, their hair lit by the sun like long rectangular halos. They could have been any girls—friends, sisters, a portrait of two girls without a history.

Her parents turned Emma's room into a workroom for her mother, boxed up her toys and clothes and sent them to the Children's Home in northern Ann Arbor. The space Emma had taken filled in quickly until there was no visible memory of her, nothing to show that Emma Fielding had for a moment occupied a small place in their world.

When Philip Fielding took a job in Santa Cruz, Allie stayed in Michigan. They had no arguments that Helen could remember. Their marriage simply slipped away as Emma had without a trace. That which had been the tangible substance of Helen's life as the first daughter of a mother and father who lived in a white clapboard shuttered house in Ann Arbor, Michigan, was gone as if it had never been.

Helen stood in the middle of the room and listened to the scratching of Gregory's paws on the hardwood floor upstairs, to the soft sound of a light wind in the bushes, a car along Main Street, the sound of a baby crying, nothing out of the ordinary. Satisfied that no one was there, she turned on the tape of "The Story of Meridian." It was Dr. Hazelton she was after—not the whitewashed man she saw on the film but the boy in the picture with her and Emma. She couldn't get him out of her mind.

The camera focuses on the back of Dr. Hazelton in his office, holding the child Molly on his lap and speaking to a woman Helen has not met. He is discussing her husband's heart condition. Molly is happily drawing on the blotter on his desk.

The narrator speaks. "Dr. Hazelton is talking to Adelaide Brown about her husband Max, who suffered a heart attack a week ago and is in intensive care in the hospital in Harrisville."

Fade to conversation between Dr. Hazelton and Adelaide.

ADELAIDE: So you have little Molly today.

Molly looks up and smiles, handing Adelaide a crayon.

MOLLY: Blue.

DR. HAZELTON: Sophie drops her by from time

to time when she's very busy so Prudential can watch her.

ADELAIDE: Such a charmer.

DR. HAZELTON (smiling): I saw Max this morning, Addie. He's doing well but no more cigarettes when he gets out of the hospital and no more corned beef on rye at the Harrisville Deli.

ADELAIDE: Max Brown doesn't listen to a word I say.

DR. HAZELTON: Well, I'll tell him tonight he's going to stay in the hospital eating soft vegetables and dry meat until he's ready to listen to you.

ADELAIDE: And no more whiskey, I hope.

DR. HAZELTON: Less whiskey, certainly.

The TV camera fades, blurs, giving the picture an evocative, grainy quality. It focuses for a moment on Molly and then on Richard Hazelton. He leans down and buries his face in Molly's hair and the camera moves out the window, along the sidewalk to Main Street where Sallie Durham is walking along alone eating an ice cream cone and, behind her, Ann Durham, her arm looped through the arm of an older woman, her mother perhaps, they look alike. They are talking although the voice is the narrator's. "It is Tuesday noon and nursery school has just let out. Ann Durham walks with her mother Alice, who grew up in Meridian, the daughter of Mr. Rubin, Sr., the undertaker—who is preparing today for the viewing of Mona Dickenson at her mother's home on Snow's Court."

Outside, Helen heard a noise, a crash, maybe a branch falling. She leaned forward, turned off the tape and listened.

It was just beside the house—footsteps, maybe an animal, but the footsteps were careful, guarded, uneven, more like those of a person. She got up from the floor where she was sitting. The person—it was a person—was behind the hydrangea bushes, next to the house, just beside the large window that looked into the living room. Helen could see that it was a woman wearing a long skirt, a small woman leaning into the hydrangea bushes for concealment.

She went to the front door. "Hello," she called.

The person stood very still and didn't answer.

Helen turned on the outside lights although it wasn't dark enough yet for artificial light.

"Hello," she said again. "Who is that?"

She had taken a step toward the figure in shadows, before she saw that it was Madeleine Sailor flattened against the bushes.

She wasn't entirely surprised.

"Don't you want to come in?" Helen asked. "I was just watching the film you gave me."

"Yes," Madeleine said, stepping into the light. "I do. I'm sorry." She followed Helen into the house.

"Were you looking for something?" Helen asked.

Madeleine folded her hands across her stomach in an awkward gesture, an attempt to seem comfortable although she clearly was not.

"I was," she said. "I was actually looking for you."

"You could have knocked," Helen said.

"Yes," she said. "Of course. I should have."

She followed Helen into the kitchen while she put on tea.

"I have very little to eat," Helen said. "Animal crackers and cereal. Blueberries. Two bananas. Anything?" she asked Madeleine.

She shook her head. "No, thank you."

Helen sat at the kitchen table and indicated that Madeleine should sit down.

"Where are you on the film?" she asked. "I noticed you watching."

"Still early, Tuesday, I think the narrator said," Helen said. "In Dr. Hazelton's office. He's with Molly."

"Oh yes. You know Molly?"

"She's been pointed out to me."

"I mean, you know about Molly?"

"I know she's Sophie's daughter and Sophie left town with her."

"Yes." Madeleine sat on the edge of the pine ladder-back chair. "That's what I meant."

She had an odd way with her lips, twisting upward as if she were smiling. "Next on the film, you see Maggie," Madeleine said. "There's Ann Durham walking along with her mother and then a very quick shot of Maggie, actually shot from behind so you don't see her face at first and then she turns and smiles."

"Would you like for me to look at it while you're here?" Helen asked.

"Yes," Madeleine said. "Yes, I would."

They went into the living room and Helen switched on the lamp, turned on the VCR.

The camera follows Ann Durham and in the corner of the screen a young leggy girl in a jacket and jeans is bending over, giving a yellow kitten a lick of her lollipop. It is a small innocent gesture charming in its simplicity.

Then the child stands and, realizing perhaps that the camera crew is filming her, she turns toward the camera and smiles, a lovely wide smile, licking the lollipop she has given the kitten.

"I play it over and over," Madeleine said, clasping her hands under her chin.

"She is a beautiful little girl," Helen said. She stood up. "Do you mind?" She turned off the VCR.

"No, of course," Madeleine said. "But next, when you look at it again, comes the drugstore with Mr. Lowry making up a prescription. Remember when I asked you to look for a clue? Have you noticed anything in watching?"

"Not so far," Helen said. "But I haven't seen enough to notice anything."

Madeleine sat twisting her skirt in her hands.

"Did you want something from me?" Helen asked. "Is that why you came?"

Madeleine looked at her, a blank look as if she had suddenly forgotten why she was there.

"You were in the bushes," Helen said. "I think you were about to look at me through the window."

"Yes," Madeleine said.

"You were?"

"Yes, I was. I was going to watch you."

"I'd rather you not do that again," Helen said coolly. "It's upsetting."

"Of course," Madeleine said. "It was wrong but I wanted to see if you were watching the film. I was afraid to knock."

"But you would have been welcome," Helen said.

"I'm sure you think I'm crazy but I have lost a sense of what is real," Madeleine said, standing uncomfortably beside the front door, fingering the lampshade on the hall table. "I ask myself is that film who we are in Meridian? Or are we who we are now, which is really quite different and a lot worse than who we used to be before the film was made." She rested her face in her hands, bending her head just slightly so as not to look at Helen. "You probably think I'm crazy, don't you? Henry does. He's very worried about me."

"I don't know you well enough to answer that," Helen said.

"No, I'm sure." She gave a little laugh. "I don't know myself well enough."

Helen took a deep breath. "Did you write a message to me in black paint on my wall last night?"

"No, I didn't. It wasn't me. David Jaspersen

asked me this morning. I said no. I couldn't do that," Madeleine said, wrapping her arms around herself. "Terrible things happen, don't they?" she said. "One minute I was in the drugstore and Maggie was outside. The next minute she was gone. That is what I mean by real. It wasn't real. It couldn't have happened except in a film but it did and it happened to me." She started toward the door. "I shouldn't keep you. I'm sure you want to eat dinner." She turned to Helen with her odd little smile. "Henry's cooking pork chops. That's all he knows to cook."

Helen watched her walk down the path to the road, down the road to Main Street and out of sight. She walked with an awkward coltish gait like a girl. For a moment Helen wanted to run down the road after her.

In her mind's eye she saw herself running. "Wait," she is shouting to Madeleine Sailor. "I know about missing children."

13.

It was late, a dusty evening, not dark, Meridian was too far north for late spring darkness to settle until after eight—but a soft gray mist hung like silk sheets on the trees and bushes. Helen had walked alone to the park where Emma disappeared.

"Disappeared" was her father's word. He never said "died" and her mother said nothing at all about Emma. Only Helen said she had died.

Disappeared because there was no body. A missing child.

"Do you think she drowned?" Helen had asked him once.

"I don't think she drowned," her father said. "Your mother does. She thinks she was swept into the larger river of which the river Meryn is a tributary."

"And what do you think?" Helen had asked.

"What difference does it make how it happened, Helen?" he said. "It happened."

"It makes a difference because I was there. I was the only one there," Helen said. "And I don't remember."

On Saturday morning T. J. had called with the news that Maggie had been spotted nearby in Lawrence at a grocery store with a man of no special description. She was wearing blue jeans and looked thinner than she had in the pictures distributed throughout Ohio and nearby states. Someone else had called later Saturday to say that a young girl matching the description of the girl in Lawrence had been seen and, for that matter, Maggie had been seen in the Meridian Park walking along the river.

"I'm going to the park," T. J. said to Helen. "Can you come?"

"I'm not finished clinic hours until four," Helen said. "You ought to go now. She'll be gone by four."

And so he went. He called later to say he was going with David Jaspersen, but by the time he got there the child had gone and the boys playing in the park, the parents of the small children on the playground had not seen anyone who matched her description.

"David says it's pretty common for people to think they've seen someone, to imagine one person is another. Projection, it's called."

"I know about projection," Helen said.

"Anyway it probably wasn't Maggie."

All afternoon during clinic hours and sore throats and a gall bladder attack, blood poisoning and stomach flu, Helen found her mind wandering to the park T. J. had mentioned where Emma had disappeared. She hadn't been there since she arrived in Meridian although she knew how to walk there by the railroad station. There was a path which led through the woods and she remembered the lush treed feel of it from childhood.

The river was high, just beneath the bank and moving swiftly, fast even for late May, almost whitewater skipping over the top. The path was narrow, laced with wildflowers, bright in the soft gray light, and thick tree roots pushed out of the earth, spread unevenly across the path, huge stones large enough to sit on right in the middle of the cleared route so she had to walk around them into the thicket. There was the dank smell of wet rotted leaves, of the river thick with bright green ferns along the bank, a wild cacophony of birds chattering.

She walked along the path toward the park, her shoulders brushing the bushes along the side, the trees leaning into the light, bending toward the sun, and in the company of abundant vegetation and especially birds. Helen didn't feel alone, although she was anxious and wished she had asked someone, maybe David Jaspersen, to come along. With human company, she wouldn't have been so attuned to her surroundings as she was now. Her memory would have been softened by the safety of conversation.

The entrance to the park was unmarked, overgrown with thick black ferns, rancid-smelling in the long heat. Helen's stomach was tight, her hands perspiring, her throat dry. She wanted to run.

In Ann Arbor she had made a point of avoiding the street where they had lived when Emma was alive—afraid the memories would do her in. A living death was what she imagined if the boxes in her brain opened and filled the tiny cranial roads with unbearable news of her past.

She walked through the dense growth, along the narrow path into a clearing which opened with a lovely, lush panorama of green fields, weekend softball players in brilliant white, families in the hushed languid attitude of late spring evenings, packing up after dinner, the smell of wood fires burning, blankets of wildflowers unfolding toward the river. The sun was just below the tree line so the evening had a sudden splash of yellow.

She knew from memory the way the wild-flowers peppered the low horizon, the heavy willows, their long-leaved skirts brushing the top of the grass, the way the river smelled and sounded at just this distance along the bank, a small steady rush of water over the rocks. The light from the summer sun dropped over the horizon, dappled the field, a pointillist configuring of soft purples and yellows and periwinkle blues, cattails near the river, high green sheaves of wheatlike vegetation, the long cry of waterfowl in the distance, a pure soft evening, a little damp and gentle, full of romance. It must have been an evening like this one, Helen thought, only a June evening after a heavy rain.

"Tell me," she asked a young boy about seven with straight square blond hair and a dimple. "Can you walk to the river from here?"

"There," he said, pointing to a slender ribbon

of clearing in the rich green velvet brush. "It's not too far but I'm not allowed."

The path to the river was narrow, and even at her height, just over five-seven, she was lost to the view of families in the open parkland. Just the top of her head showed above the high sheaves. A child would be invisible here, she thought, and she wondered did her parents allow her at five years old to walk unseen by grownups for such a distance along a path that led to a river. A small child with her baby sister, almost three, three in October. What could they have been thinking? she asked herself, walking out of view of the open field where her parents must have been sitting on the benches around the picnic table.

She is walking with Emma. The sun on its way down in the western horizon falls as the sun seems to do in the evening, dampness in the air promising rain.

Her mother had told her she was a talker when she was small. Always in a story of her own device, taking on the major roles, her mind crowded with narrative possibilities. She didn't remember an imaginative mind—it must have fallen away years ago, replaced by an affection for the specific and literal, for things seen—but a sense of her young mind came back to her now.

"We have to hurry to the river, Em," she is saying. And that is what she called her sister. Em. Not Emma.

"We have to make a pony ride and the ponies

will be gone soon. There'll be children for us to play with and animals."

"I can't hurry," Emma says. "I'm too little."

"I'll carry you then," Helen says, lifting her plump baby sister in her own small arms.

"You can be my mama," Emma says happily.

"I am your mama," Helen says. "I am your good mama.

"Here they all are, Em. See. Down at the river waiting for us with lemon cakes and chocolate chip cookies," Helen says. "You can have one cookie and half a lemon cake and yummy mint tea with honey."

The path opened to a grassy bank with birch trees and huge oaks and willows hanging lazily over the river and large rocks down to water which ran surprisingly clear.

Helen leaned against a slender young birch which gave a little with her body, bending away from her.

This was a place where she had been before. There were no specific identifying marks. No rock formations or land cuts or odd designs of trees that she remembered, and she didn't know why she was certain. But she was.

14.

Helen called T. J. from the rail station on the way home from the park.

"Any more news?" she asked, hoping to seem offhand although she had a reason for the call.

"None," he said. "I think the news about Maggie was bogus."

"But you have to follow any leads, I suppose."

"I feel as if I do," he said. "I did see Madeleine and Henry tonight. I believe she's slipped over the edge."

"Had she been drinking?" Helen asked. "That's what I noticed when she last came by my office, but earlier she stopped over at the house and didn't seem drunk, just odd."

"Crazy?"

"She did, a little."

"That's what Henry says," T. J. said. "He pulled me aside and said he was terribly worried she was losing her grip."

Helen wanted to ask T. J. to come over, to sit around the half-lit living room, half lit to keep her from seeing where the writing on the wall had been. She wanted to watch the film but not alone. It had taken on a quality of menace and she wasn't sure whether that came from the film or whether the menace had to do with the real Meridian.

She was fragile after her visit to the park and, in spite of T. J. Wisely's frank sexuality, he was safer to her with his eye patch and wheelchair, somehow clearer in aspect than David Jaspersen with whom she knew she could easily fall into the thing she always fell into with men, a love affair, embers before she had a chance at something genuine. A love affair wouldn't happen with T. J. He was walled in, as she was. She couldn't get at him. They were equals in that way and, in her life with men which had been as considerable as it was slight, she had never been with a man who seemed familiar as kin.

"Where are you?" T. J. asked. "You sound as if you're outside."

"I'm at a phone booth by the rail station," she said. "I was out for a walk and just decided to call." She caught her breath. "Would you like to stop by?" she asked. "I was thinking of watching the rest of the film."

There was a long pause.

"Maybe you've seen the film enough times," Helen said.

"No," T. J. said but she sensed that he was tentative. "There're scenes on the third cassette from the wake of a young woman who happened to die while the film crew was in town and they actually filmed her wake. Have you seen that part?"

"I haven't," Helen said.
"I'll be over," T. J. said.

Helen made pasta, rotelli with a little cheese, no sauce, there was very little in the fridge. But there was a bottle of white wine and half a baguette from lunch and blueberries, so they sat on the gray couch, Gregory between them, the film playing, the sound slightly muted so they could talk.

"Mona died of cancer," T. J. said. "It started in her breast."

Tommy Dickenson moves across the screen, walking down the line of mourners, kissing one and then the other. He shakes hands with T. J., then hugs him, takes Mona's golden retriever by the collar and leads her, in her black ribbon and white rose, up to the front porch where she stands with Mona's mother and sister in the receiving line.

"Mona Dickenson was twenty-seven," the narrator is saying. "She was lovely and talented, a pianist of real promise who studied in New York and had a generous quality of spirit, an angel, so her best friend Madeleine Sailor describes her." The camera focuses on Madeleine standing in line next to Henry with Maggie, who is distracted, her back to the camera, leaning against her mother.

T. J. was pensive.

"She used to play at First Methodist and the

sound honest to God broke my heart." He took a cigarette out of his pocket. "I was in love with her." He put the cigarette in his mouth. "Don't worry. I'm not going to light it."

"What is going on with the dog?" Helen asked.

"You'll see what the director does with the dog at the end of the scene," T. J. said. "But here, I don't know. I was in another part of the yard. Peter Forester may have said to Tommy, 'Go get the dog. We want to shoot him standing with the family of the deceased.' Something touching like that." He lifted Gregory on his lap. "My quibble with this film—I shouldn't tell you. I should have you make up your own mind."

"No, tell me," Helen said.

"My quibble has to do with reality. How when you take a little truth and misconstrue it—" T. J. lifted his legs and rested them on the coffee table. "I'm not talking about making up a story. Stories are orderly. What I'm talking about is fussing with the facts to make something better than it is or different, so who knows in the end what's real and what's not." He poured himself another glass of wine.

"It doesn't really seem to be about the town you know?" Helen asked, trying to wind her way into T. J. Wisely's confidence but she wasn't sure of herself the way she usually was when eliciting the stories of other people's lives so they felt an unrequited intimacy with her.

T. J. shrugged.

He fast-forwarded to the end of the scene at

Mona Dickenson's wake, the frame of the dog lying on the front porch, a shadowed outline of Mona's casket in the window behind her.

"That's what I mean," he said. "That scene is sentimental. The film crew shouldn't have been at the wake. They didn't know what to make of a real young woman dying in a small town where everybody knew her and so they made something sentimental because the truth is too complicated for television, too ambiguous." He finished his glass of wine. "Now I get mixed up between the town and the story about it."

"It wouldn't be a film without a story," Helen said, taking off her shoes, slipping her feet under her long skirt.

"A town isn't a story," T. J. said. He fast-forwarded the film and stopped at a frame of Sophie DeLaurentis dancing with Peter Forester.

"Do you know who she is?"

"She's Sophie."

"What have you heard about her?" T. J. asked.

"That she bolted just after the film."

"Nobody has said anything about her?" T. J. turned off the light in order to see the film better.

"When I first came, I went on house calls with Prudential and everybody asked had she heard from Sophie." Helen took his plate, poured them both another glass of wine.

"And Prudential said no."

"Prudential said nothing," Helen said. "Who's Sophie with there?" she asked, pointing to Peter

Forester, his cheek pressed against Sophie's full black hair. "I haven't seen him before."

"That's Peter Forester, the director, dancing with Sophie." He clicked the rewind button on the television monitor, returning to Mona Dickenson's wake. "Sophie DeLaurentis from Alliance, New Jersey, knows zilcho about Meridian and she is the star of his documentary."

Helen leaned back against the couch pillows, putting her feet on the coffee table.

"There's something I don't understand about you and this film," Helen said.

He broke apart the cigarette he'd been holding, scattering the tobacco in a plate on the coffee table, took another out of the pack in his pocket. "I wanted to honor Meridian because for me, growing up, it was a safe house. And something went wrong."

The camera crew follows the Sailors home after Mona Dickenson's wake, filming at a long distance and from behind. Henry Sailor is walking a little ahead, holding Maggie's hand, Madeleine, willowy and walking at an angle, a little to the left. Maggie stops, pulling her hand free from her father, and turns toward the camera, suddenly self-conscious. She covers her face with her hand and turns away, her arm around her mother's waist, her head burrowing into the side of her. There is no music and the narrator is silent, only the sounds of nature superimposed, bird song, the rustling of small branches, the swish of early spring wind blowing Madeleine Sailor's coat in the direction in which she's walking.

"That's Maggie," Helen said.

"Yes," T. J. said. He stopped the film, rewound and replayed the scene with the Sailors. "That scene rings true," he said.

"Was Maggie your favorite?"

"The reason I'm putting so much time into finding Maggie is that I'm responsible," T. J. said, replaying the frame with the Sailors. "I brought the film crew to Meridian in the first place and the film brought the tourists who wanted to come to see us for themselves, and one of them must have taken Maggie." He pulled his wheelchair over and moved off the couch into the seat. "My fault she's gone, if you understand."

"I do understand," Helen said and she wanted to say more. She wanted to say that she understood fault exactly. For a moment she thought she would tell him about Emma, but the moment passed and she went into the kitchen to make coffee.

"Don't make coffee for me," T. J. called. "I should go."

"Do you have to leave?" Helen asked, leaning against the doorframe.

"It's late." He turned on the lamp. "Why?"

She shrugged.

"Are you afraid here?" He had a look on his face, a kind of sweetness, and she wanted to say something truthful to him, something undefended about herself. "I can't tell whether I'm afraid to be alone in this house because of someone else," she said, "or I'm afraid to be alone with myself."

He asked her why she had come to Meridian, since certainly there were other places to go.

"I like emergencies," she said.

"But the emergency is over, isn't it?" he asked.

"Legionella is over. At least, it's not an emergency."

"Then go back to Ann Arbor," T. J. said. He said it kindly. "We're not a good place for a visiting physician."

"What do you mean?"

He shrugged. "I'm a fatalist," he said. "Sometimes it's the wrong time and the wrong place."

She helped him wheel his chair down the few front steps of her house. "Are you all right going home in the dark?" she asked.

"I'm fine," he said.

"You didn't do the writing on my wall, did you? Suggesting I go home?"

He laughed. "No," he said, touching her lightly on the waist. "I told you that face to face."

It was late but light enough for Helen to see his shadowed figure wheeling up the narrow street, keeping a grip on the wheels so they did not spin backward, and she was stirred by the power in his arms.

V.

VISUAL MEMORY

The Story of

Merdian

Thursday, April 12

Dr. Hazelton was up all night before the fourth day of shooting of "Meridian." Sandra Doyle had a baby girl by caesarean section just after 1 A.M. at Harrisville Hospital, and by the time he returned to his house there was a message on his answering machine from Tommy McCollough with a bellyache which turned out to be a bleeding ulcer. When he got back to Meridian a second time from Harrisville, it was 7 A.M. and Sophie was sitting on the top step of his front porch with Molly sleeping in her arms.

Her long black coat was open and she was dressed for an evening in the city, in a blue wool dress, cut quite low, too tight across her breasts, her hair loose and curly around her face, her face bright with rouge, red on her lips, on her cheeks, her eyes circled in black mascara, a pout on her full lips.

He was fragile from exhaustion and tense, his emotions flying. When he saw Sophie, he wanted to kill her.

"Is that what you wear to bed with the director?" He could not help himself.

"Rich." She gave him a little-girl look. "This is business for me. I could have a career." She put a sleeping Molly over her shoulder. "Peter says I might be discovered when people see the film." Her voice went suddenly soft with pleasure. "He thinks I'm talented."

"That you certainly are," Richard said. "Talented especially. Anyone can see that."

"I've come with Molly," she said. "She has a fever so I knew it would be best if Pru took care of her while I'm working."

"A fever?" He opened the front door and held it for her to go inside. "How high?"

"I don't have a thermometer at home," Sophie said.

"You have a three-year-old child and no thermometer?"

"I lost it," Sophie said. She put Molly down on the couch while Dr. Hazelton took her temperature.

"I have to be on the set early," she said. "Eight-thirty, Peter said."

"The set? So now Meridian is a set?" He checked the thermometer. "A hundred and three."

"Oh dear." Sophie was distracted. "Not exactly a set," she said, "but you know what I mean. This morning they're staging a dance sort of like the one we have in the grammar school every Christmas."

"I said her temperature is a hundred and three."

Molly had started to cry. She sat up on the sofa, her small hands covering her face.

"I knew there was something the matter," Sophie said. "What do you think?"

"I don't know." He was exasperated. "I haven't checked."

"Well, it's eight-fifteen and I thought I'd leave her with you now to check over and then when the shoot is over I'll come back and get her." She picked Molly up and kissed her. "I think it's a virus. Didn't Sallie Durham have a virus last week?"

"Not that I know of." Dr. Hazelton washed his hands. "I'll be at the office with her after nine. If you finish on your set before then, I'll be here," he said coolly. "Should you fancy checking on her."

"Don't be mean, Richard. This could be a break for me." She turned to leave. "You know I've never taken help from you or anyone else. I've raised Molly alone."

"Who knows?" Richard said. "You pass yourself around like a plate of sugar cookies."

But she had gone down the steps, no longer listening, rushing toward Main Street in her slender high-heeled shoes. Molly was crying, her eyes wide, calling after her mother, and the crying put Richard Hazelton in a sudden rage.

"Hush," he said to her.

"I want to get my mama," she said.

"We'll get your mama," Richard Hazelton said. "We'll get her on the double right now."

He saw himself behind the wheel of his yellow Toyota sailing down Main Street after Sophie DeLaurentis in her tight blue dress, sailing over her, down she goes, under the car, flat as a blue sheet on the road.

Almost blind with fury, he picked Molly up, rushing out the front door to the car parked in the driveway. He put her in the front seat, pushed the door shut although it must not have caught, and ran around the back of the car, jumping into the driver's seat, turning on the engine, putting the car in reverse.

It happened in a second, before the car had reached the bottom of the driveway. The front door of the Toyota was open and Molly was no longer in the car. He had not even felt the door fly open—when the car in reverse was going down the driveway.

T. J. Wisely was sitting with Peter Forester, dressed in a dark blue suit and tie, and Pleeper Jones when Sophie came in the diner, went over to the counter and ordered coffee black and plain toast.

"The Christmas dance is not a big deal," he was saying to Peter. "I thought the whole point of this film was the story of the real town—not made-up Christmas dances in the middle of April."

"We need a diversion, some sort of party. A picnic on the river doesn't work in April," Peter said. "The trees are still in bud—people are still in jackets. But a dance does."

"You're dressed for the occasion," T. J. said, ordering more coffee. "I didn't know you owned a tie."

"I don't," Peter said. "The tie belongs to the undertaker and the suit is the chief of police's." This seemed to please him.

"I suppose you plan to be at the dance because of your long personal association with Meridian," T. J. said. "A crowd scene is what you have in mind?"

"I plan to be at the dance because it amuses me to appear in my own work." He leaned across the table and tweaked T. J.'s nose. "And, T. J., I'm the director."

Sophie slid in between T. J. and Peter with her breakfast.

"Dieting?" T. J. asked.

"Peter said I might take off some weight," she said, tearing her dry toast in little pieces. "A person looks heavier on film than in real life, right, Peter?"

"That's right, Sophia," Peter said.

"So when do I set up?" Pleeper asked.

"Now," Peter said. "We're doing the dance first thing this morning because we've got the town meeting later and a church supper at the Methodist church."

"So the whole dance deal is made up," T. J.

said. "That pisses me off, Peter. If I had known you were going to misconstrue the truth this much, I would have suggested Hollywood."

"Listen, T. J., you'll be happy with this film, and the Christmas dance is not my invention. It's Meridian's. I'm making use of what is already here." He followed Pleeper out of the diner, ruffling Sophie's hair as he passed. "You look terrific," he said.

T. J. ordered more coffee. "Sophie," he began.

"Leave me alone, T. J. I have problems."

"I can see you do." He looked at the shoot schedule which Pleeper had left on the table.

7:30 A.M.	DANCE SHOOT. Duncans, Durhams, Sellerses, Sophie (Peter), Brownlees, Fosters, Evans, Grahams, etc. (Story line with Peter and Sophie.)
10 A.M.	TOWN MEETING at Meridian Grammar School on subject of flood control and rat problem
11 A.M.	CATHOLIC LADIES GUILD preparation for St. Patrick's Day Snake Dinner
12 P.M.	LUNCH at the diner. Focus on Ben Winters
12:30 P.M.	Follow Sophie with Molly to the cemetery on the

anniversary of her husband's death

1:00 P.M. 2nd grade ball game at the grammar school.

"I see you're taking flowers to the cemetery, Soph. Peach glads and carnations, it says, provided special for the occasion by Bill's Florists. Very nice."

"I'm not kidding, T. J.," Sophie said. "This morning Molly had a high fever and I was up most of the night with her so I'm not interested in your making fun of me."

"I'm not making fun of you, Soph," T. J. said wearily. "I just don't understand how in good conscience you can take flowers to Mr. DeLaurentis's grave in front of a TV crew when you've never done it unattended. Besides"—he took out a cigarette—"I didn't even think you liked him."

"If you weren't a cripple, I'd slap you." She drank the rest of her coffee, left $1.25 on the table and went out the back door of the diner, up the hill to the high school where they were filming the Christmas dance.

Edith Winters was on her way up the hill with her baby girl on her shoulders and Sophie called out to her. "Slow down," she said. "I can hardly walk in these high heels."

"Hello, Sophie," Edith said.

"Are you doing the dance part of the film?" Sophie asked. "That's why I'm so dressed up."

"Benjamin just told me about the dance this morning," Edith said.

"I know you don't think much of this project."

"How do you know?" Edith asked edgily.

"Everybody knows. Peter told me."

"Peter?"

"Peter Forester. You know, the director. He's living in your house." They waved at Mrs. Walker, standing on the front porch of her cottage talking to the postman as they passed.

"He's living in the church hall," Edith said. "Not my house."

"You don't like what's going on, isn't that so?" Sophie asked.

"I think the film is changing people," Edith said quietly. "And I don't like change."

"But we'll be famous, Edie," Sophie said.

"I hope not," Edith said. "I can't think of anything worse."

It was going to be a cool wet April day, a little windy, hovering gray clouds, a distant pale yellow sun. Sophie pulled up the collar of her coat.

David Jaspersen saw T. J. wheeling up the hill and ran to catch up with him.

"I hear the Christmas dance is scheduled for this morning," he said.

"Sure," T. J. said. "I hope you can make it."

"Did I see Sophie here a minute ago?"

"You did," T. J. said. "On her way to fame and fortune, into the arms of Peter Forester."

"Peter Forester's in the shooting today. He's wearing my suit," David said.

"Yes, he is," T. J. said. "Playing the role of the stranger from another town visiting the Meridian dance."

David pushed T. J.'s wheelchair the rest of the way up the hill. "You know, I'm getting very concerned."

"You are!" T. J. said.

"I had a call this morning from *Hometown* magazine saying they wanted to do a story and then *Good Housekeeping* called saying they'd heard about the film."

"It's almost over," T. J. said. "They finish up tomorrow night. They'll be out of here by Saturday morning and we can go back to normal."

"Not a chance we'll go back to normal," David said.

Peter Forester had worked out a story for the dance.

It is Christmas. Sophie is a widow, alone with a child, and Peter, a stranger, a visiting uncle of the Durhams from Chicago. They meet at the dance. No conversation between them. Peter sees Sophie. She is dancing with Sam Durham. Ann Durham tells Peter about Sophie—how she married Antonio DeLaurentis and he died months before Molly was born. Peter cuts in on Sam and dances with Sophie. As the small story progresses through the dance section, there are frames of Sophie and Peter. They do not speak but each frame shows them moving closer together.

"So what's the conclusion of this sweet story?" T. J. asked Pleeper Jones, sitting on the sidelines in the lunchroom decorated for Christmas. "Together forever?"

"Not cool," Pleeper says. "They dance. They say good-bye. The stranger leaves and Sophie returns to life as usual."

"Dumb plan," T. J. said.

"I just shoot the picture," Pleeper said. "I don't worry about the plans."

"I don't get why you did that," T. J. said to Peter after the shooting, on their way to the town meeting in the grammar school auditorium.

"You're getting too excited, T. J.," Peter said. "The trouble with filming what's real is that it misses the spirit of the place. The spirit is in invention and not in fact. Which is why I did the story of a momentary romance."

"I know that," T. J. said. "I have no problem understanding the business of making things up. It's just important which stories you choose to invent."

David Jaspersen sat in his office with Win in his pajamas wrapped up in a blanket, sitting on the hard seat across from his father reading a comic with a thermometer in his mouth. David took the thermometer out.

"Normal," he said to Win, who didn't look up from his comic. "How bad do you feel?"

"Bad," Win said.

"Is your throat sore?" David asked.

Win nodded yes. Yes as well to a headache and stomachache and achy muscles.

"So I suppose we should see Dr. Hazelton," David said.

"Maybe," Win replied.

Prudential answered when David called.

"He's not here," she said.

"It's nine-thirty."

"I know what time it is," Prudential said.

"Maybe he's at the hospital."

"I called the hospital," Prudential said. "He hasn't been there yet this morning and he's not at home."

"I'm calling about Win," David said.

"A lot of people have been calling this morning with children who say they're too sick to go to school but haven't got a fever and no symptoms," Prudential said. "I call it Meridian Flu-A strain. Too many cameras in town."

David laughed. "Well, have Rich call me when he gets in," he said and then, reconsidering, redialed the clinic. "And, Pru, if he doesn't come in pretty soon, call me."

He went over and sat down next to Win.

"Other children have the same illness in your class," he said. "I was just speaking to Prudential."

"So?"

"What's going on in your class?"

"A sickness," Win said.

"No, Win. I wonder what is really going on. Are you sick with a real sickness or has something happened to make you not want to go to school?"

"I feel sick," Win said. "Everywhere."

"But has something happened at school?"

Win looked up over his comic book at his father. "A little something," he said.

"What is it?"

"They said I was too small."

"Who is they?" David asked, taking hold of Win's foot affectionately.

"The film people."

"And what did they say you are too small to do?"

"Too small for basketball. Today they are filming a game between the two second grades and they said me and Ricky Martin and John Freemont and Paley Rivers are too small and Oliver Bent is too uncoordinated and Billy Fisher still has the chicken pox on his face." He had started to cry. "Also," he said, "I can't be in the whole school picture."

"What do you mean, you can't be in the whole school picture?"

"I wasn't chosen."

"But it's the whole school."

"Only some people were chosen. It's not really the whole school but it's supposed to feel like it is."

David shook his head.

"I'm certainly glad they're leaving tomorrow."
"Me too," Win said.

Ben Winters stood in the center of the church hall with the assistant director and the cameraman, discussing the filming of the church supper.

They had to remove the cots set up for the film crew, bring the tables out, set up a stage for the Sunday school original musical called *Mercy, Be Kind to the Indians* with Sallie Durham and Molly DeLaurentis playing the nonspeaking parts of Chippewa children and Major Rivers playing an Ohio pioneer with Sara Peace playing his wife Mercy. The crew from the high school was finishing the set of a reservation, covering the flats, lined with blue-black pine trees, a slate-gray lake winding through.

"We'll need about a hundred people," the cameraman was saying. "Any more and I won't be able to move around."

"So explain to me how this will go," Ben Winters asked.

"We'll start around six," the assistant director said. "What would normally happen if this were a church supper evening?"

"People arrive—not just the Methodists—when we have our monthly supper, everybody comes. A lot of people. Well, not everybody, of course, but it's nondenominational. In fact the churches are really community centers for people," Ben said, noticing that he was being recorded. "People come less for God than to mingle around a big living room together." He was pleased with the sound of what he said.

"And then you speak?"

"I usually say a prayer of some kind and I'll make a welcome."

"We'll be following some of the stories of people we've been concentrating on in the last few days—Sophie and Molly, the Durhams—we've been doing a few things with Prudential and she's great on film. Will she be here tonight?"

"You never know with Prudential. She can't be pushed."

"And we'll be doing David Jaspersen as the good cop."

"He's actually a lawyer," Ben said. "Trained in Madison."

"I didn't know," the assistant director said, interested in the information. "Why did he change professions?"

"He's never said but this is his hometown and he wanted to come back."

"I can certainly understand that," the assistant director said. "It's a dream of a town. I wish it were mine."

"Yes," Ben said, filled with a sense of personal victory. "It really is."

He wanted to tell the assistant director his story in Meridian, how he had been born in Oshkosh, Wisconsin, and his father was a drunk and then he'd met Edith, who was a girl when he met her, really a child, but the assistant director was in a hurry to meet the rest of the crew at the town meeting on flood control.

"Later," he said, putting a hand on Ben's arm. "I'd love to hear about it later, Reverend."

Ben surveyed the large assembly room, his room, his place, his church, a small simple white Methodist church in a corner of Ohio, hardly a dot on the detailed map of the United States. Reverend Benjamin Winters, rector, age forty-two, five-eleven, a hundred and forty-eight pounds, fair, thinning hair but no gray yet. People all over the United States, watching television in their living rooms or dens or kitchens, would know First Methodist, Meridian, would know Reverend Ben Winters and his wife Edie and their baby daughter. They would see this room, hear his voice. If he happened to be on vacation in Chicago or Miami or Seattle, people might recognize him on the street and say, "Look, that's the minister from the Methodist church in the film 'The Story of Meridian.' "

He could hardly contain his excitement. He had to be called to several times before he heard Sam Daily from the high school, who was painting the set, shouting for a mop.

"We spilled some paint on the stage, Reverend Winters," Sam called. "Could we borrow a mop?"

"Sure," Ben said. "Of course. I'll get it." He headed to the large kitchen where the broom closet was, still imagining himself on film—

"Here is Reverend Winters," the narrator might say, "busy with the details of his daily life as rector of First Methodist, attentive always to matters small as well as matters large." He opened the swinging door and there on the linoleum floor by the stove and lying in a small heap was a child, on her side, facing away from him, in navy-blue tights and a yellow jacket with the hood up.

15.

On Thursday morning Prudential called in sick. There was a message on the machine when Helen arrived at the clinic just after seven and, when she tried to call Prudential's house, there was no answer. She sat down at the desk and dialed T. J., who was sleeping.

"I'm sorry to call so early," she said, "I'm looking for Prudential. I need to know where she lives."

"Why?" he asked.

"Because she's not here and not answering the phone and I have to have help at the clinic today."

She could hear T. J. stretch and yawn, perhaps he was sitting up in bed before he spoke. "I'm sorry," he said. "I can't tell you where Prudential lives."

"That's crazy," Helen said. "This is a small town."

"She doesn't want people to know," T. J. said.

"Everyone in town knows where Prudential lives, T. J." Helen said. "People don't want me to know."

"She lives way out of town," T. J. said.

Helen checked through the patient list for Thursday—eleven appointments, with a lot of possible clinic walk-ins. She phoned David Jaspersen.

"Prudential called in sick this morning," she said, "and today's going to be busy."

"If you need it, I'll find you some help. I'm on my way over to the clinic now," David said. "Did you sleep better last night? No invaders?"

"I slept fine," Helen said.

Although it didn't seem as though she had slept at all. The bedroom at Dr. Hazelton's house had a smell from home. A smell of Mackinaw, maybe of her mother. A fresh-water smell. "Cucumber" was written on the clear cologne her mother kept on the shelf behind the toilet at Mrs. Peaches's guesthouse. After T. J. had left the night before, Helen hadn't been able to sleep. There was a chill in the air and the smell of cold made her uneasy, like weather change when the outcome is unpredictable.

She had dreams of smothering, face down, someplace soft with the thick damp river smell of Meridian. She couldn't turn her head or lift it, struggling for breath. When she was awake enough to take a breath, a gulp of air, she realized she'd been dreaming about her parents at the river on the evening that Emma died.

Her mother had been thirty, her age almost exactly, her father thirty-three—a handsome athletic couple, taken with each other, pleased with their place in the world. She had seen pictures. Her mother was lovely in a simple vibrant way. Her father was long-legged, slender with a wonderful open face and good bones.

What had her parents been doing that evening at a picnic in the river park? she wondered. Why had Helen been allowed to walk that long path of high wildflowers? She and Emma must have been out of sight for some time, invisible to the grownups sitting around the picnic tables. They were small and moved slowly, maybe even picking flowers as they walked.

Were her parents worried, she wondered, or didn't they even notice she'd been gone so long?

Helen had just hung up the telephone with Mrs. Walker, sick with the stomach flu, and was collecting the charts for the morning appointments, when David walked in the clinic.

"Henry Sailor called me," he said. "Madeleine never came home last night. He's on his way over here."

People had seen Madeleine. Ann Durham had seen her Sunday downtown on Main across from the library talking to someone from one of the tour buses.

"A bus from Cleveland," Sam Durham said. "I saw the sign on the front."

Tom Walker, Maria's father, had seen her in the pharmacy talking to a woman with bluish permed hair dressed in navy-blue spandex and a white shirt, an older woman with a loud voice. She had gone into the pharmacy with the woman, who was a stranger to Meridian, probably from the tour bus, to buy over-the-counter sleeping pills. They seemed to know each other.

"I don't know what to say," Henry said, sinking down on the couch in Helen's office. "She left early yesterday and called me at the grammar school to cook dinner because she had a late appointment with you," he said.

"I didn't have an appointment with her," Helen said. "The other day I discovered her looking in my living-room window while I was watching television, but I haven't seen her since."

Henry looked up. "Crazy," he said quietly. "Is that what you think?"

"Distraught is what I think," Helen said.

"What about the people on the tour bus?" David asked. "I hear she goes down in the afternoon and talks to the people from the buses."

"She's been doing that," Henry said. "She goes around lunchtime to see if anyone is parked at the church clock and then she strikes up a conversation." He leaned back in his chair wearily. "I'm sure she's hoping someone will know about Maggie."

"Are you suggesting she could have left with a tour bus?" David asked.

"I don't know what I'm suggesting," he said.

He looked ancient to Helen, sitting with his side to the long window behind her desk so a shaft of morning sunlight painted his face a sickly yellow with lines too deep for the face of a young man.

"David"—he leaned toward David's chair and his voice had a disturbing urgency—"We're disintegrating."

"What did he mean, disintegrating?" Helen asked later after Henry had left.

"Henry believes we shouldn't have allowed the film to be made," David said, "because strangers have started to come since they saw us on TV." He put on his cap and opened the door to the clinic. "It has to do with Maggie."

"But what he said seemed personal," Helen said. "It was directed at you."

"I don't know what he could have meant then," David said coolly. "A man under emotional duress can't be counted on for sense."

The clinic was filling with patients, sitting quietly with magazines or books, their arms folded across their chests, their eyes closed.

"It looks like you have a full day," David said. "Would you like to have dinner?"

She shook her head. "I put the Blake baby in

the hospital with pneumonia early this morning. I have to work late."

Helen followed him to the front door, walking out on the porch of the clinic so the patients sitting in the waiting room wouldn't hear her. "Why can't you tell me where Prudential lives?"

"You didn't ask me," David said, pulling away, redefining the borders of their friendship.

"Can you tell me where she lives?" she asked.

David hesitated. "Ask her," he said.

"She won't tell me," Helen said crossly. "Prudential never talks."

Win Jaspersen came by at lunchtime, looking for his father, he said. He sat at the desk across from Helen while she ate lunch between patients.

"You could move into our house if you don't like Dr. Hazelton's," he said. "We have an extra room."

"Thank you very much," Helen said. "But I think I have to stay in Dr. Hazelton's house. It's been given to me for the time I'm visiting here."

Win folded his arms across his chest. "I didn't like Dr. Hazelton," he said.

"You didn't?" Helen said, eating the tomatoes and turkey out of her sandwich.

He shook his head.

"How come?" she asked.

"He gave me the creeps. He had a bad temper." Win shrugged.

"Did he ever lose his temper at you?" Helen asked.

"I saw him lose it once at Sophie," Win said. "I was waiting for a strep test and he lost his temper right here in the waiting room."

"Sophie?" Helen got up, threw out her trash from lunch, took out the files. "I haven't met her yet."

"She doesn't live here anymore. Dr. Hazelton moved too, of course. That's why you're here. Right?"

"He moved because he had a family emergency."

"Nobody told me that," Win said. "He had a cat," Win said, drawing a cat on a prescription pad.

"I know," Helen said. "Named Gregory. He lives with me now."

"I'm allergic to cats."

He moved over closer to Helen, leaning his chin on his hands.

"Are you married?" he asked.

"No, I'm not," Helen said.

"Neither is my dad," he said.

"So he told me," Helen said, checking the clock. She ruffled Win's blond hair. "I have to start clinic hours now, Win, so you'd better go," she said, taking Win's hand, walking him to the door, waving good-bye as he went across the street, where T. J. was wheeling his chair into the ice cream store.

Late in the afternoon Helen called Prudential. It had been a day of ordinary complaints, stomach flus, earaches, a case of strep, a kidney infection, no indication of a new case of legionella. Perhaps if the weather held and there was no more flooding, the epidemic was finished.

Prudential was distracted.

"You heard about Madeleine Sailor?" Helen asked.

"She's lost her marbles plain as day."

"Well, I'm going to borrow Reverend Winters's car and check the hospital and I'll do a run of house calls," Helen said. "Certainly I'll stop by the Durhams' and maybe the Walkers'."

"I'll come with you," Prudential said. "I'll be there in half an hour."

Her father called while Helen was cleaning up the examining rooms. He was cheerful with a familiar false gaiety in his voice, asking how she was and how her work was going, saying he was off on holiday to Belize and wished she could join him but knew she was too busy. And then, as if there had been a sudden shift in emotional altitude, his voice dropped to a lower register, the cheer gone out of it.

"I spoke this morning to your mother," he said. "She thought we should tell you that on the day Emma disappeared we were having a little celebration in the park. It was our wedding anniversary."

"Why didn't she call me herself?" Helen asked.

"You know your mother, Helen. She doesn't like the telephone."

Helen sank into the swivel chair at her desk.

"What are you trying to say to me, Daddy?"

"It's your mother's idea," he said, uncomfortable with this conversation. "She called last night to say that perhaps you didn't know we'd been having a celebration that afternoon."

"I didn't," Helen said. "You've never told me anything about that afternoon."

"It's upsetting to have you back in Meridian, Helen," her father said. "Your mother can't help being nervous about it and I suppose we feel it's almost intentional on your part."

"It is intentional," she said, but she didn't want an argument with her father. Her life felt too slippery to risk the slim hold she had on her parents. So she changed the subject to a discussion of the symptoms of legionella, which seemed to please him, and then she got easily off the phone, resting her head in her hand, trying to catch her breath which had gone suddenly out of her.

A sunny dappled day in late June, champagne-colored as summer days in the northern Middle West can be. In the distance, Helen sees her parents, their heads together, hears their silvery laughter. She cannot get their attention.

"Mama." She goes over to the picnic table and tugs on her mother's soft silky skirt. "I want to go to the river to see the birds."

Her mother, whispering with her father, does not look down.

"Take Emma for a walk," she says or maybe it's her father speaking. "Be careful of Emma."

"Go down the wildflower path to the river. Bring your mama a bouquet of yellow flowers for her anniversary."

Has she made that up? Helen thought. Was her sudden memory playing tricks—the mind dusting off its unalphabetized stories in the brain?

"Now?" she asks.

"Please," her mama says. "Take Emma's hand and pick me lovely flowers."

She goes off down the path with Emma's hand in hers, looking back to see if they are paying attention, if they see her going off. But they don't. Their faces close, their fingers laced, drinking pale yellow champagne, kissing and kissing.

"Good-bye, Mama," Helen calls. "Good-bye, Papa."

But they don't hear her.

Prudential arrived in a temper.

"So let's get out of here," she said. "I don't have all day."

"Are you better?" Helen asked, gathering up her things, her medical bags, a light sweater, pinning her hair back.

Prudential gave her a look. "Better than what?"

In Reverend Winters's car, the women didn't speak, Helen conscious of Prudential's unembarrassed concentration on her as they drove across Highway 15 in the pale orange sunset. She was conscious of the size of Prudential, who though tall was not an indelicate woman. But today she seemed enormous.

"Were you actually sick this morning?" Helen asked.

"No," Prudential said casually. "Why?"

Helen laughed. "Because you said you were."

"Nothing's the way it seems." Prudential folded her hands around her knees, pulling at the hem of her long skirt.

"I suppose," Helen said. She would have liked to talk to Prudential about things that mattered, although she knew Prudential would, like her mother, refuse. But not like her mother either. Silence was a matter of choice with Prudential and, with her mother, it was more like destiny. Sitting in the car next to this woman who seemed to be larger than her actual size, seemed to take up the whole front seat, Helen had a kind of certainty, as if there were unspoken personal conversations between them, no reason to imagine a genuine relationship. But she did.

"I put Nellie Blake in the hospital," Helen was saying. "She has a little pneumonia and she's too tiny to take a risk like that."

Prudential's head was turned away now, watching out the passenger window at the blanket of yellow wheat. It was a pleasant bright late afternoon, a freshness in the air, a whisper of cool, and Helen had a sense of well-being, even high spirits which had to do with Prudential in the car beside her. Perhaps, she thought, their chemistry was in common like two large dogs who simply smell right to each other.

"What do you think about Madeleine Sailor?" Helen asked.

"I'm not thinking about her."

"But if you were, do you think she's gone off with one of the tour buses?"

"She could have."

"Do you think she's crazy?"

"I think she's playing at being crazy so folks will let her alone with her sorrow," Prudential said. "That's what I'd do in her place."

"I have a question to ask you," Helen began, risking intimacy.

"Don't ask a lot of questions," Prudential said. "We get along good enough as friends."

They stopped by Nellie Blake's room and Nellie was already improved on an antibiotic drip and then they checked on Mr. Marquez, who was well enough to be discharged. They stopped in the hospital cafeteria in the hospital's basement, a green room of long Formica tables with weary doctors bending over their plastic trays, an eerie quiet. They ordered two chocolate milkshakes, drinking in comfortable silence.

"Do you like David Jaspersen?" Helen asked finally.

"Enough."

"I mean do you trust him?"

"Trust?" Prudential gave the subject consideration, lifting her head at an angle. "I don't trust anyone." She took a pen from behind her ear and wrote something on a note pad she kept in her pocket. "Are you thinking of marrying him?"

Helen laughed. "Not likely," she said.

Prudential sat with her shoulders hunched, two fingers like pencils against the high bone of her cheek, her eyes scanning the room suspiciously as if she had reason to expect someone concealing an automatic weapon to materialize. She drank slowly, stopping to stir, to lick the other end of her straw. From time to time she looked at Helen so directly that Helen looked away.

"It looks as if this epidemic is under control with erythromycin," Helen said.

"Uh-huh," Prudential said. "It does look that way."

"So if it's over there's no reason for me to stay on." Helen began hoping for a reaction, for affirmation, a request from Prudential to remain in Meridian. "You needed an emergency doctor, that's all. Isn't that right?"

"After the flood we needed an emergency doctor. That's right." She looked at Helen, her eyes half closed. "So leave."

"I don't want to leave if there's a real need for me," Helen began. "But I had only intended to come as a visiting physician to take care of an emergency situation." She took her glasses off and put them in her pocket. "If you were in my position, would you leave?" she asked.

Prudential shrugged. "I'm not in your position."

"People here seem to want me to leave," Helen said, brushing against the parameters of conversation.

Prudential rested her chin in her hands. "When I was thirteen—young, young, young"—she shook her head—"I had a baby die on me and it was my fault," she said. "You can't say if I were in your position because you are you and I am me and different people in the same position are still different people."

"But you have an opinion."

"My opinion is this," she said matter-of-factly. "I wouldn't leave a place where the children are in danger, and the children in this town are in danger from more than dirty water."

On the drive home Helen wanted to talk, to ask about the baby who died and whether it had been Prudential's own baby. And if it was her baby, how had she found herself with a baby so young? She wanted to know the details of its death and whether it was a boy or girl and was Prudential responsible as a result of carelessness or had it been unavoidable. But Prudential had closed the curtain on conversation.

Helen glanced at her picking her teeth.

"Is it because of the baby dying that you became a nurse?" she asked, turning off Route 15 into a Texaco station.

"I'm not a nurse," Prudential said.

When the car stopped, she got out and went to the public telephone at one end of the filling station. Helen watched her lope across the road, dragging one leg just slightly as if she had had a small stroke. She picked up the phone and leaned against the kiosk. Helen loved the way Prudential moved with grace in spite of her limp, the way she tilted her head just so as if she were lifting an ear to the world so all its troubles could pour in.

And where did that rush of feeling come from? she wondered, her detailed and scientific mind grinding through land mines of emotion.

Prudential climbed back in the car and shut the door. "I had to call home," she said. She had a package of caramels which she opened, offering one to Helen, crossing one leg over the other, lacing her long fingers together.

"Who was at home?" Helen asked.

"I thought your job was answers," Prudential said.

"I'm a young doctor," she said. "I have to ask questions."

It was dusk. The warm air blew between the open windows in a low song, softening their voices, and she felt the weight of Prudential next to her, the long sapling size of her, her dancing brain locked in its skull box buzzing like the sparks off electric wires strung along the road. She wanted a confessional.

"I was wondering," Helen began, ignoring Prudential's comment, pulling out onto the road. "What happened to the baby who died?"

Prudential gave her a look.

Helen couldn't see the look but she could imagine what it was and she didn't continue. What she would have said if Prudential had been willing, what she would say in time, maybe even tonight, was "No wonder we are friends. We have a common history."

And then she'd tell her the story of Emma.

"Who says we're friends?" Prudential would say, knowing all the time that of course they were friends. Their friendship was certain, traveling the air between them like the scent of smoke.

Helen drove along Route 15 through Aimsville, slowed by an Amish wagon outside of Baertown, taking a left off 15 into Meridian, traveling on the narrow road beside the railroad tracks.

"Look out," Prudential said.

"Look out?" Helen asked. "For what? I don't see anything."

"Look out not to knock over Madeleine Sailor walking along the road."

Madeleine Sailor was walking slowly, picking wildflowers beside the road, and what Helen saw was Madeleine holding the hand of a small girl with curly hair who was wearing a short pinafore and no shoes.

"Shouldn't I stop?"

"No," Prudential said. "She might run off if you stop and surprise her. We'll send David Jaspersen after her as soon as we get in town."

Helen gripped the wheel on the windy road, looking in her rearview mirror as the road turned, and she lost sight of Madeleine behind the curve.

But just before she turned, following the road, she caught a glimpse through the mist of the child walking along with a bunch of flowers in one hand and holding the hand of Madeleine with the other. She hadn't seen her for years, a lifetime of days and hours and weeks, but there along the same paths of Meridian where Helen had lost her was Emma Fielding.

16.

Helen stopped the car at the police department. It was warm, a light breeze lifting her skirt, the air sweetly perfumed. As a child, she used to look into the mirror over the sink at Mrs. Peaches's guesthouse until her face lost its familiarity, and now, looking at her hands, her long-fingered slender hands around the steering wheel, she didn't recognize them as belonging to her.

She wanted to ask Prudential about the child with Madeleine Sailor. She wanted to know was it a vision or a real child? And could she count on Prudential? Perhaps Prudential hadn't seen her because she looked too quickly. Perhaps she wouldn't tell the truth. She was selective about what she saw and what she didn't see.

"I'll tell David about Madeleine." Prudential climbed out of the front seat, putting her long legs out first, stretching when she stood up. "You go on. He'll take me home."

"I'll wait and take you," Helen said, not wishing to be alone as if, without a witness to her presence, she was in danger of disappearing.

"Another time," Prudential said casually but Helen knew it wasn't casual.

She leaned in the window, resting her arms on the car door, sticking her head in so she could hear above the sound of the engine.

"I was wondering," Helen began, trying to appear calm. "When you saw Madeleine walking along the road just now, what did you actually see?"

"I saw Madeleine Sailor walking along the road," Prudential said.

"Describe it," Helen said. "I just got a glimpse out of the rearview mirror. Was she picking wild-flowers?"

"Not that I noticed," Prudential said. "She was walking along the side of the road and in no hurry and she was wearing a blue and white checked skirt with buttons down the front and a white T-shirt and her hair was rumpled. That's what I saw."

"Oh well." Helen smiled, running her fingers through her long hair, fallen from its knot on the top of her head. "I guess I was wrong about the wildflowers."

She didn't mention the child, although certainly she had seen one. Prudential must have also seen the child, clear as day, a small chubby little girl wearing a pale yellow dress Helen didn't remember on Emma although the face and hair were Emma's. And even if she had imagined the identity of the child out of urgency and desire, she could not have imagined a child where no one existed unless she had lost her mind.

She dropped Ben Winters's car at the church, dropped the keys in the mailbox and walked up the hill, a little breathless although the hill was small.

The house was dark. Gregory was lying on the front stoop and pinned to the door was a note.

I came by. I need to speak to you pronto. News on Maggie. T. J.

She crushed the note in her hand and tossed it in the wastepaper basket in the hall. Gregory followed her from the hall to the living room to the kitchen; an uneasy tomcat, his long black and white tail twitching in the air, lacing through her legs as she opened the fridge—which was full again, a carton of orange juice and cranraspberry, a loaf of whole wheat, sliced turkey and fresh tomatoes, celery and carrots in a plastic container, a carton of 2% milk, a plate covered in aluminum foil with a note from Edith Winters.

"In case you haven't eaten," the note said, and Helen felt a twinge of anger that her house was open to anyone in town; her wall could be defiled, her refrigerator filled. After all, who was to say she wanted 2% milk, and maybe she was a vegetarian. The note had an arrow and she turned it over.

*I need to speak with you as soon as possible. Call 863-*2143. Edie Winters.

Helen didn't wish to speak with anyone. Something was happening. She felt herself slipping, as if the person inside her body was insubstantial and she was losing herself. If there had been no child walking along the road with Madeleine Sailor, then she was hallucinating children.

"I need an emergency," she had told her mother in her senior year in high school when, because the rooming house was full, they had spent the summer in the same room.

"You need a boyfriend," Allie Fielding had said. "A boyfriend feels like an emergency."

"No, Mama, I have a boyfriend. That's easy. I always have a boyfriend if I want." And it was easy—young men wanted Helen—something about her, some promise in her carriage. An agreeable distance. No demands.

"I mean I need a life of emergencies," Helen said. "If nothing is required of me I'll disappear."

"I know," Allie Fielding had said softly.

"How do you know?" Helen had asked, surprised at the confessional tone of her mother's conversation. "I have always thought you wanted a life without emergencies."

"I don't want an emergency," Allie had said.

"But I know what it means to feel so empty you can't imagine filling the hole," she'd said. "Only I'd rather disappear."

It was a moment, maybe the only moment, in which Helen could remember the space between her mother and herself close over, heal like an open cut.

She took off the aluminum foil and ate the cold baked chicken and ratatouille and dill potatoes from Edie Winters, standing up.

Perhaps the food was poisoned, she thought. Not the chicken necessarily. That would be difficult. But a little something in the ratatouille, she decided, not unhappily, feeling some small pleasure in Gregory as he wove between her ankles, his soft fur a kind of comfort.

The phone rang and she let it ring, listening for the voice on the answering machine, that of David Jaspersen. And she picked up.

"You sound upset," he said.

"I've been poisoned," Helen said.

"Poisoned?"

"Cyanide in ratatouille from Edie Winters," Helen said. "By the time you get here I'll be dead."

"Helen," David said, unamused.

"This is my first experience with paranoia," she said.

"Are you afraid to stay there tonight? Do you want to be with us again?"

"I'm fine," Helen said. "Did you pick up Madeleine?"

"We took her home," David said. "Prudential went with me."

"Where had she been?"

"Drinking," David said. "She went as far as Harrisville on one of the tour buses and then went into a bar."

"She was alone when you picked her up?" Helen asked, the picture of the child clear in her mind.

"Someone had dropped her off at the Route 15 turnoff," he said. "She was very much alone."

"Oh well," Helen began, not knowing how to finish the thought.

"I might stop over later," David said.

"Actually, I'm exhausted."

"And you're sure you're not afraid?"

"I'm not afraid," she laughed. "Just turning a little crazy in this postcard-perfect small town."

There were calls on her answering machine and after she hung up with David she played them.

The first was from Edith Winters.

"Checking to see if you're back yet and have eaten," she said cheerily. "I hope to speak with you tonight. Call any time," she said, emphasizing "any time."

The second was her mother. "Hi, sweetheart. It's me. Four-fifteen. Could you call as soon as possible? I need to speak with you."

Helen called but there was no one at home,

just the soft voice of her mother on the answering machine, as usual. She wasn't going to call Edith Winters. She turned off the downstairs lights, picked up a compliant Gregory and went upstairs. In her bedroom, she took out her medical dictionary.

> *Depersonalization Disorder is an emotional disorder in which there is a loss of the feeling of personal identity. The body may not feel like one's own and important events may be watched with detachment. It is common in some forms of schizophrenia and in severe depression.*

She had felt this way before. One afternoon living with Oliver while he was a resident in surgery, she had come home from the hospital early to find him asleep next to the jigsaw puzzle she had had made for him from a photograph of herself. The face was almost finished except for a triangle that included the temple, a portion of forehead and the right eye—so the total effect was disturbing, as if the reproduction of her face with its triangular hole was exact. Automatically, she had reached up to feel if a part of her head was missing.

She had awakened him.

"I'm afraid something's the matter with me," she said, holding her head which had no feeling when she touched it. "Am I all right?"

"How would I know, Helen?" Oliver said, not pleased with excesses of emotion.

"I seem to have lost feeling in my head." She showed him the part of her head and face replicated in the jigsaw.

He checked her eyes, her reflexes, took her pulse.

"I'm hallucinating," Helen had said.

"You're overtired," Oliver said. "Take a nap."

She tried to sleep. But every time she closed her eyes she felt a huge space where her forehead ought to be and she couldn't fall asleep.

Often she was plagued by a palpable sense of loss, as if parts of her actual body were in the process of disappearing. Now, sitting on Dr. Richard Hazelton's double bed, she was missing large parts of herself, her arms between her shoulders and her hands, wide empty cavities in her brain, only the small memory of Emma walking along the road to Meridian, a perfect miniature, in the corner of her mind.

Downstairs, she turned on the VCR, putting in the fourth cassette, which opens with children walking to school all over town, down Main Street, and Aspen and Euclid, spilling out of their houses in ones and twos and threes, kissing their mothers on the small front porches of the brightly colored modest Victorian clapboard houses which pepper the Meridian hills. It is the morning of the performance of *Snow White* at the grammar school and the children, walking and skipping, arms laced together, whispering at the street corners, roughhousing on the lawns, are in high spirits. The film is in slow motion, capturing the dance of children playing, their wide-open smiles in slow motion; it moves up Poplar Street to Molly DeLaurentis's house where Molly sits alone on the front porch with a fat stuffed kitten on her lap, her purple mittens on either cheek, her eyes wide. She is waiting, looking off in the direction of the village so she doesn't see Sallie Durham flying down the hill in her bright red jacket, her long hair braided, her cheeks chapped pink. She collides with Molly on the porch and they fall into each other's arms like puppies, kissing and kissing in delight.

She didn't hear T. J. arrive. She hadn't actually fallen asleep with the film of "Meridian" spinning pictures of children but her sense of awareness was so close at hand, so self-conscious, that the outside world was muted in comparison. When she did hear him call to her and realized he was knocking, she leaped out of her chair.

"You frightened me," she said, sitting at the bottom of the steps, wrapping her arms around her legs.

"I'm sorry," T. J. said. "I knocked a couple of times. I guess you were sleeping."

"I was sleeping," Helen said.

T. J. was in shorts, his pale legs loose and dangly like the legs of a child, his eye patch comically askew. "Are you okay?"

"Don't I look okay?" Helen asked, susceptible to suggestions. "I think I'm fine. I hope I am."

"Are you watching the film?"

"I was and then I must have fallen asleep," she said.

"I left a note," T. J. said.

"I got the note," Helen said. "I was so tired I didn't bother to try to call you."

"The news is bad," he said.

She followed him into the kitchen.

"Do you have milk?" he asked. He opened the refrigerator and took out the quart of milk. "I had a call this evening from a woman who works in a gas station in Baertown who saw the newsbreak on Maggie and she thinks she saw her in a car with a pale skinny well-dressed man with a baseball cap on backward."

"You say the news is bad?"

"The woman pumped gas and, while she was doing the windshield of his car, she saw the child lying on the front seat." He poured milk and looked in the cabinet, finding a box of crackers. "She thought the child looked dead."

Helen shook her head.

"A man isn't going to stop in a gas station with a dead child on the front seat, T. J. He'd be crazy."

"I know, but it's the third time I've gotten a call from a person nearby who has seen her." He took bread out of the fridge. "I'm always hungry when I'm nervous. Could I make myself some toast?" he asked. "Jam?" He checked the door of the fridge, taking out a jar. "Edie's own raspberry, not bad."

They were at the kitchen table when David Jaspersen arrived, knocking at the front door, walking in without waiting for anyone to answer. He got a glass of water.

"I'm sorry to barge in like this," he said, checking his watch. "There've been a million things happening tonight."

"Anything about Maggie?" T. J. asked.

"Not about Maggie."

"I had a call from Baertown from a woman who said she saw Maggie lying on the front seat of a car driven by a well-dressed youngish man."

"Dead," Helen said.

David took half a piece of toast from T. J.'s plate. "I got that call too. Not a possibility."

"But it's the third call I've gotten from someone in the vicinity of Meridian who's seen her," T. J. said.

David shook his head. "How many calls do you get a day?"

"Two hundred," T. J. said.

"They've seen her pictures on television. Maybe they've seen 'The Story of Meridian.' It's a miracle you don't get two thousand calls a day." David looked in the fridge. "Do you have a beer?"

"No," she said, going into the living room, stretching out on the couch. "Just half a bottle of wine."

He came into the living room, drinking straight from the bottle, sitting down on a ladder-back chair next to the couch where Helen was lying.

"You seem a wreck," Helen said.

"It's been a hard day." He pulled a notebook out of his pocket. "Five-fifteen P.M. corner of Aspen and Rowder, Billy Blake lost his temper and hit Callie Blake. Five twenty-seven while I am at Callie Blake's, I receive a call on my beeper that Henry Sailor on his way to the pharmacist's house to get some sleeping pills for Madeleine, which she shouldn't have because she's still drunk, slammed his car into Toby Oler's parked car on Main." He finished the wine and put the empty bottle beside his chair. "And Toby, who was just going into the movies when it happened and is by nature a quiet even-tempered man—I played football with him and know—lost his temper, swung at Henry and told him he was going to kill him."

"Jesus," T. J. said.

"You're under a lot of pressure with the sick children," Helen said. "It's not entirely surprising."

David was silent.

"That's part of it," T. J. said.

"I used to be clear about things," David said. "Rules were rules. Things like that." He stood up and crossed the room. "Who knows what's true and not true any longer? Certainly not me," he said, genuine anger in his voice. "You, T. J.?"

"Shut up, David," T. J. said.

"Please," Helen said. "This has been a very long week."

David turned on the television. "Do you have the film?" he asked.

"It's in the VCR," Helen said.

The channel flickered from zigzag lines to salt and pepper, finally surfacing on a picture of Dr. Richard Hazelton walking down the street holding the hand of Molly DeLaurentis and another child Helen didn't recognize.

"Who is that man?" David asked, indicating Dr. Hazelton assuming the pose of an actor.

"Isn't it Dr. Hazelton?" Helen asked, a little frightened at the suddenness of his outburst.

"Exactly. Dr. Richard Hazelton, late of Meridian, Ohio," he said. "But who is he really?"

"Cut it out, David," T. J. said. "Pull yourself together."

"No, no. Listen to me. I'm saying something important, something philosophical. Is this man the good quiet, pale-faced physician we recognize as one of our own or is he someone else?"

"This is not about the film, David," T. J. said. "What's the matter in Meridian we've done to ourselves."

"I don't know that," David said, turning off his beeper, which was ringing. "I don't know a thing." He picked up the phone on the side table. "Mind if I use your phone?" He dialed.

"Prudential?" He listened.

"I'll be right down," he said.

"Has something happened to her?" T. J. asked, alarmed.

"Prudential's fine," David said, heading toward the front door.

"Do you need me?" Helen asked, sitting up.

"I don't," David said. "It's not that kind of problem. It's personal."

"I'm sorry about all that," T. J. said after David had left. "Sometimes David has a temper."

"Everybody is very much on edge," Helen said.

"That's true," T. J. said. "It's been a difficult spring and then this illness," he said but Helen knew it wasn't the fault of legionella.

After T. J. left, Helen turned off all the lights and sat in the dark in the living room in case a person with a mind to harming her should throw something through the window that faced the front of the house, a large double window with no curtains or shutters or blinds.

When she called her mother, the answering machine was on with her mother's voice. But she had a sense of someone there behind the machine. She could see her mother in her blue jeans and a red bandanna around her head, weaving tapestries. Was she still weaving tapestries in New York City, did they have any interest for a city dweller or were they collecting dust rolled up in the back of a closet in her apartment?

She called her father, who said he'd call back after yoga class.

"Don't bother," she said. "I want to talk to you now. Not after you do yoga. After you do yoga, I may be dead."

There was a long pause.

"Don't be extreme, Helen."

"I'm not extreme. I'm serious. Why doesn't Mother ever answer the phone? You call. Tell her I'm sitting here waiting for her to call me. And do it before yoga."

"I will," her father said quietly. "I'll do it now."

He called back immediately, too soon to have made the call, and waited for the answering machine to complete its information.

"She's out," he said. "I'm sure she'll call you when she gets back home."

Helen waited. She counted to twenty-five. And slowly, she counted to one hundred as her mother used to make her do when she was a child, impatient for time to pass quickly. Then she dialed her mother's apartment again. This time the message had the voice of a man, her stepfather certainly. "You have reached 684-6050. Please leave a message and we will get back to you as soon as possible," he said.

Now her mother wouldn't even allow Helen to hear the sound of her voice.

One more time, she dialed New York. When the message beeper sounded she said in a cool and even-tempered voice, "Mother, this is Helen." She was going to say, "I hate you," in the same cucumber voice, but she couldn't bring herself to do it.

She was six, in Mrs. Dawn's first grade in Mackinaw, and Mrs. Dawn had a baby so Helen refused to go to school with a substitute until she returned.

"You have to go to school, Helen," her mother said at breakfast at Mrs. Peaches's. "I'm taking you to school now."

"I won't go," Helen said.

"You will," her mother said.

"No," Helen said, but she knew the fight was already over and she had lost it.

"I hate you," she said when her mother took her hand and walked with her out the front door. And as they crossed the threshold of Mrs. Peaches's guesthouse it seemed as if the walls fell in, the roof slid into the street and all around them Mackinaw was burning.

When a call came later, Helen thought it was her mother, letting it ring before she answered so as not to seem too eager. But it wasn't her mother.

"I'm calling to ask you to come on over," Prudential said as if it were a normal invitation from an ordinary friend. "I've roasted a chicken."

"It's late," Helen said. "You're sure?"

"I eat late," Prudential said, giving Helen directions to her house. "It's not a long walk from your place."

In the kitchen Helen fed Gregory and finished off the wine, even wishing there were more of it left to quiet her nerves. She wasn't exactly afraid, not enough to refuse the invitation, but she was certainly uneasy.

VI.
Do No Harm

The Story of

Merdian

Friday, April 13

The fifth day of shooting "The Story of Meridian" was a Friday and the last day because the budget was tight and Peter Forester had only allowed for five days of camera crews. He was known in the industry for economy in the use of time. But without the weekend, he had to make special arrangements to set up weekend activities on Friday—church services and ball games and club meetings. It was complicated, particularly church services on Friday, which meant the shops had to close for a while and the schools miss a day of classes so half of Friday could be Saturday and half could be Sunday.

On Friday morning Peter was in a terrible temper. He came late to the morning meeting in the coffee shop before the shoot. Pleeper was already there with the rest of the film crew and his assistant. David Jaspersen was there and T. J., Ben Winters, which was unusual for the minister of First Methodist, and Sophie looking dreadful, her eyes puffed and red, the whites veiny, her color pallid.

"What is the matter with you this morning?" Peter asked Sophie, coming in the back door with a cigarette. "You look like the wrath of God."

"She has the flu," David said.

"Great. Good news. Hours to wrap up and the star's sick."

"It's not my fault," Sophie said quietly, her life entirely altered since Thursday evening.

"I'm sorry. I'm sorry." He took hold of her wrist absent-mindedly. "My patience is thin today. You'll have to excuse me."

" 'S okay," Sophie said. She had lost interest in her film career, so exhausted she could hardly sit on a chair without falling.

"So today we do church in the morning and sports in the afternoon. I'll need a pile of people dressing up for church. School's out, isn't it?" he asked. "You've let school out?"

"It's out," David said.

"First I'm doing the clinic thing I didn't get to do yesterday with Molly," he said.

"You'll have to choose another child," T. J. said evenly.

"I've been tracking Molly. I want to stick to these few familiars. I've got a story going."

"Then do Sallie Durham. You've been following her," T. J. said.

"What's with Molly?" he asked.

"Molly has the flu."

"And, Peter," David began, ordering more coffee and doughnuts all around, "if you're doing the clinic, it will have to be with Prudential because Dr. Hazelton had to leave on a family emergency."

"What?"

"He had to leave," T. J. said. "It was an emergency."

"Shit," Peter said. He leaned over to Sophie and touched her hand. "Don't worry about me, Sophie. I'm a bear on wrap-up day. It's not personal."

Sophie didn't reply.

"Are you okay?" Peter asked her, looking over the schedule with Pleeper.

"Fine," she said. "I'm fine."

By Thursday early evening, Dr. Richard Hazelton had left Meridian, called out of town on a family emergency, the message for Prudential on the clinic answering machine said. But Prudential already knew and so did most everybody else.

Dr. Hazelton drove directly north from Meridian into Michigan, around the waistband of Lake Michigan into the Upper Peninsula, where he checked into a Motel 6. He bought the Friday papers and a stack of mysteries and moved into Room 110 overlooking a parking lot and then the town of Elksville. He had no plans, only a vague notion that he would drop his identity in Motel 6. Or maybe not. Maybe he would return to Meridian, depending on Molly.

Dr. Hazelton realized almost immediately at the bottom of the driveway before he turned toward

Main Street that the front door of his Toyota was open and Molly was gone. He stopped the car, got out and dragged himself up the hill to his house, sick with fear. She was lying on the side of the driveway and when he knelt down beside her, his angel, his own, something snapped in his brain.

Molly was unconscious. She had fallen on her head, on the side of her head, although there was no mark. He put her gently in the back seat of the car and drove to the church hall where the film crew was staying, carrying her down the back steps to the kitchen. What he had in mind—in his fractured mind—was a confrontation with Peter Forester and the film crew.

"This is what you have done to my child," he was going to say to them, say to Peter Forester, holding Molly toward them in his long outstretched arms. "You have ruined our lives."

He opened the door and was just walking across the linoleum floor, past the stove and the long table, when he heard someone coming, someone on the other side of the kitchen door, and in a panic, his brain scrambled, he laid Molly gently, gently on the floor and ran. Soon, he thought, driving back to his house, they would pay and pay and pay—the director and the film crew and Sophie DeLaurentis with her cotton-candy dreams.

When Reverend Ben Winters discovered Molly, he assumed she was dead. His first thought as he rushed up to his office with her was that she'd been murdered, maybe raped and murdered by a member of the film crew. He laid her on the couch in the corner of his office, covered her with a blanket, turned off the light, locked the door and rushed downstairs to find David Jaspersen.

Edith saw him first.

"Ben," she said, catching a glimpse of his bone-white face as he rushed by. "What's the matter?"

"Nothing really," he said. "We have a bit of a problem and I need to find David." He grabbed her wrist. "Don't make an issue. It's important with the film crew here to keep up face."

David was dancing with Sophie after the supper, high stepping to Sam Durham's fiddle, and Sophie had her head turned, camera ready.

"I have to go pick up Molly at the clinic," Sophie was saying. "She has a virus but first Rosie Doyle is going to do my hair because Peter wants to do just a couple more shots of me that got messed up. I thought I'd have Rosie do it prissy."

"Whose idea?" David said.

"Peter's," Sophie said demurely.

Peter had come into the church hall with Pleeper, going over the late evening's events.

"Now, Sophie," he began.

"Sophie has to go get Molly," David said for her. "Molly has the flu. But I need to talk with you."

"I have another shoot with Sophie and Molly at Mr. DeLaurentis's grave, so I hope she's okay."

"She'll be fine," Sophie said, hurrying off across the room, disappearing in the crowd of high school students.

"I was talking to my son this morning, Peter," David said. "And he's very upset that you are doing a whole school picture without the whole school."

"You know about film, Chief. I can't do the whole school," Peter said. "There're too many and it wouldn't be aesthetically pleasing to have so many." He slapped his clipboard nervously against his thigh. "The picture of the school will appear several times throughout the series as a leitmotif and I want it to look attractive, not a mob scene." He put his hand on David's arm. "I'll have your son included."

"That's not the point," David said.

"I get the point, David, but I'm a filmmaker, not Dr. Feelgood, so I'm going to do what looks good." He turned away. "You'll be glad. By May, Meridian, Ohio, will be a household name."

David Jaspersen was just walking out the back door of the church hall in a temper when Reverend Winters intercepted him.

"She's not dead," David said, standing up beside the couch in Ben's office after he had examined Molly.

"She's unconscious?" Ben said.

"Yes, but I don't know enough to say anything

more." He picked up the telephone and called Prudential.

"Dr. Hazelton isn't here," Prudential said. "He hasn't come back."

"I thought Molly was with you."

"Not with me," Prudential said. "Dr. Hazelton never came to afternoon clinic hours at all."

They—Edith holding Molly—drove the patrol car to the clinic, which was almost empty. Only Prudential was there. Sophie hadn't yet arrived.

Prudential was standing outside when they drove up.

"There's a message on the answering machine," she said. "Dr. Hazelton's been called away on a family emergency."

"Then who was Molly with?" Edith asked, carrying Molly through the waiting room to the back examining room, laying her on the table where Prudential checked her pulse, her eyes, her air passage, unbuttoned her pale blue corduroy dress.

"She obviously hit her head, although I don't see a mark," she said. "We have to get her to Harrisville."

"What do you think, Pru?" Edith asked.

"I don't know what to think," Prudential said. She telephoned the hospital.

"You didn't talk to Dr. Hazelton all day?" Edie asked. "Isn't that odd?"

"More than odd," Prudential said.

"Doesn't Sophie sometimes leave Molly with Dr. Hazelton?"

"She does," Prudential said. "He brings her here for the day. He likes to have her around."

Ben Winters sat on a chair, his head in his hand. "I was afraid something like this might happen," he said.

"Like what?" Edith asked anxiously. "What is this like?"

"Like an accident," Ben Winters said. "When you get careless, there's an accident."

"It's not an accident to find a child lying unconscious in a kitchen," Prudential said.

"We have to find Sophie and get to the hospital," Edith said.

"Did you call T. J., Prudential?" David asked.

"You call T. J.," Prudential said. "He's still at the church hall is my guess."

"I'll call him," Edith said. "And then I'll get Sophie."

"She's not at home," David said. "I called the beauty parlor and she's not there. She's having her hair done at Rosie's and Rosie Doyle doesn't have a phone."

"I'll go to Rosie's," Edith said.

In the back seat of the patrol car on the way to the Harrisville Hospital, Sophie sobbed.

"At seven this morning I took her to Rich's," she said. "He was going to take care of her and then take her to the clinic."

"Was Rich in a bad mood when you dropped her by?" David said.

"A little," Sophie said. "He was a little bad-tempered."

"Someone brought her to the kitchen of the church hall," David said quietly. "She couldn't have come alone."

"Ben thinks it might be someone from the film crew," T. J. said.

"I don't think so, T. J.," David said. "Sophie left her with Rich and what we know about Richard Hazelton is that he's careful to a fault. He wouldn't have let her out of his sight."

"What do you think, Sophie?" T. J. asked.

"Is there any reason to think that Rich could have done something to Molly?" David asked.

"Like what?" Sophie asked. "What do you think could have happened to her?"

"An accident," David said. "Something accidental, and then he panicked and lost his senses."

"How well do you know him?" T. J. asked.

"I don't know," Sophie said. "I sort of know him."

"Sophie?" David began but she was crying now, uncontrollably.

"Don't be mad," she said. "Please, T. J., don't be mad at me."

"Nobody's mad, Sophie."

"Prudential's mad. You're mad at me, aren't you, Prudential?"

"Mad is not the word," Prudential said.

"Rich was mad this morning," Sophie said but

only T. J., sitting next to her, could hear her clearly. "He was mad about the film because Molly is in it," she said. And then, almost under her breath, "He thinks Molly is his," she said.

"Is she?" T. J. asked. "Is she his child?" Perhaps the unfamiliar brusqueness of his voice alarmed her.

"Maybe," Sophie said, weeping. "Maybe. I'm not sure."

David sat with T. J. and Prudential in a small room at the Harrisville Hospital waiting for the doctor.

"Are you bowled over?" T. J. asked.

"No, not bowled over," David said. "I never thought of it before—I never thought Rich Hazelton could—but Antonio was pretty sick to be making babies that last year and it does explain Rich's visit to me the other morning."

"Jesus," T. J. said, shaking his head.

"Nothing like television to bring out the truth," David said.

"The truth about what?" T. J. said. "Sophie isn't really from Meridian." He turned to Prudential, who was reading the newspaper. "Are you surprised?" he asked.

"I'm too old for surprises," she said.

Edith and Benjamin Winters arrived before the doctor. It had started to rain, a cold black rain, and they were soaking.

"Do we know anything?" Ben asked.

"We know this," David said and he told the Winterses about Sophia and Dr. Hazelton.

"What are we going to do?" David said.

"What's to decide?" Prudential asked. "We send the police after Dr. Hazelton and tell the film crew to move their sweet bottoms out of this town."

"No, Pru," David said. "That's not how we're going to do it."

Ben Winters sat in the metal chair, his hands together. "I think we're going to keep it a secret," he said.

"Keep what a secret?" Edith Winters said.

"What happened to Molly."

"Why would we keep it a secret?" Prudential asked.

Ben Winters lowered his voice, speaking as if people were listening in the next room. "A child found unconscious in the church hall." He shook his head. "Absolutely not. They'll film this," he said, indicating the door to the room where Molly was being examined. "We'll be known everywhere as the place where a thing like this can happen."

"This isn't the right way to go about it," Prudential said. "I don't like it at all."

"It's the moral thing to do."

"Moral?" Edie said. "I don't understand you, Ben Winters. What's moral about telling a lie?"

"We're not telling a lie. We're not telling anything," Ben said, standing now, in charge of the situation. "We're protecting our town."

Prudential shook her head. "I'm going home to South Carolina by the weekend," she said. "This isn't a place for a decent person to live."

David folded his arms across his chest, leaned against the door.

"Ben is right," he said, surprised at his own calmness. "We'll get together tonight at my house after the film crew's gone to bed, someone from every house involved in the filming."

"And what are we going to say to the film crew about what happened?" Edie asked.

"Nothing. We'll say nothing," David said. "Dr. Hazelton has been called away on a family emergency. Molly has the flu."

The doctor came into the waiting room with Sophie, who sat in a chair on the other side of the room, turning away from them, facing the window.

"I believe she simply hit her head falling from a distance," Dr. Bartoli said. "You just found her on the sidewalk, is that right?"

"That's right," David said.

Prudential slid deep into the blue plastic couch on which she was sitting and closed her eyes.

"It's a head injury, a broken arm and possible internal injuries. She has lapsed into a coma—on the Glasgow coma scale." He showed them the motor responses. "Not good but not the worst by any means."

* * *

Riding back from the hospital to Meridian, T. J. in the front seat, David was sick with nerves. He turned off 15 into Meridian.

"I used to be so sure of what I thought and I've lost that," he said.

"Who doesn't lose it?" T. J. asked.

"Worse than that. I'm about to do something which I know is wrong and I'm going to do it anyway."

"You're the chief of police protecting your town."

"I ought to go after Richard Hazelton. That's the law."

"So?"

"I'm not going to do it."

There were thirty people at David Jaspersen's house at midnight. The news had slipped by osmosis into the houses of Meridian like an airborne virus carried by the winds. People spoke in low voices, worried that their conversation could be heard seven blocks south at the church hall where the CBS film crew was sleeping.

"What is our story then?" Ann Durham asked.

"That Molly has pneumonia."

"What about Sophie?" Edie asked.

"She's at the hospital now," David said. "But she'll be here tomorrow to do the filming."

"Peter Forester seems to have fallen in love with Sophie," Sam Durham said.

"I've worked with Peter Forester for a few

years," T. J. said. "What you've been observing is called lust."

"Sophie might tell," Henry Sailor said. "She's human."

"She won't tell," David said. "She promised and she's terrified of what will happen."

"What will happen?" Edie asked. "I mean what will ultimately happen after the film crew leaves?"

"What do you mean, happen?" David asked.

"Richard Hazelton must know something," Madeleine said. "You'll try to find him, won't you?"

"Rich has been called away on a family emergency," David said. He hesitated. "I have no reason to go after him."

"He was taking care of Molly," Madeleine said. "He was the last person to see her."

"We don't know that," David said.

"As if that makes any difference," Madeleine Sailor said quietly from the corner of the room where she was sitting on the floor.

"What do you mean, Madeleine?" David asked.

"I just don't like lies," she said. "They grow. I've seen them grow fat with blood like wood ticks."

"This isn't a lie," T. J. said. "It's a concealment."

"I don't like concealments either," Madeleine said. "Something will happen."

"You have to make these kinds of choices,"

Mr. Rubin, Sr., said. "Though I certainly understand your concern, Madeleine. I'm concerned too. The film crew wanted to come into the funeral home when Mona was being fixed up Tuesday. They're not entirely likable."

"But the point is what do we do about this?" Sam Durham said. "And what we do is protect ourselves."

"This is the lesser of two evils," Henry Sailor said. "Always my father used to tell me, choose the lesser of two evils."

"Our lips are sealed," Henry Sailor said to David, who stood at the back door of his house, embracing his fellows, his childhood friends, watching them wind into the dark moonless night.

"What do you think?" T. J. asked, lighting a cigarette, after everyone had left.

"I don't know what I think," David said, sinking onto the living-room couch.

On Friday they filmed church school in the rooms the film crew had been using, classrooms with large round tables and small chairs.

"I want Molly," Sallie Durham pouted. "I don't want to sit with Maria and Tommy Blake. He hits."

"Molly's sick," Ann Durham said to her. "You'll be fine, darling." She turned to Peter Forester. "How do you plan to do this?" she asked.

"I'm trying to capture the children thinking about ethical questions," Peter said, "like what is the meaning of family or what is death or what is good and bad—the adults will be talking about the same thing, so we'll have a sense that in this community important things matter." He picked Sallie up and put her on the edge of the table. "What happens in your Sunday school classes?"

"We have a story like 'The Good Samaritan' and children relate the story to their own lives," Ann Durham said. "Even children small as Sallie."

"I'm trying to get across that your lives are more substantive, more humanistic, less materialistic than the lives of most Americans."

"We live good lives," Ann said. "I know that sounds unsophisticated but we are a kind of tribe and careful of one another."

Sallie looked up at Peter Forester suspiciously.

"Molly got run over by a car," she said in the middle of their conversation.

"Molly what?" Peter asked.

"Molly has the flu, Sallie," Ann Durham said. "Remember I told you?"

Sallie closed her eyes.

"Daddy said that Molly got run over," Sallie said after Peter Forester had gone to the other side of the church hall.

Peter Forester slipped his arm over Sophie's shoulder.

"I really want to do that shoot at the cemetery, Sophie. Do you have something black to wear—maybe that long coat of yours and very little makeup? The gray light today will give your face a nice color and you ought to look pale."

"Okay," Sophie said.

"Right after the Sunday school shoot, I'll do you walking from your house with the flowers—and then wherever your husband's buried, I want you to pass by Mona Dickenson's grave. You can put one flower of yours on her grave, then go on to your husband's grave." He was pensive for a moment. "What do you think about the dog following you there—Mona's yellow dog?"

Sophie looked perplexed.

"Following me?"

"Never mind," he said. "Probably a dumb idea."

Benjamin Winters arrived at the church hall in full dress.

"Is everybody going to be at church?" Peter asked.

"Everyone was notified," Ben Winters said. "They'll be here."

"Do you have a sermon prepared for this?" Peter Forester asked.

"I have an old sermon about grace."

"Grace—that's a big seller," Peter Forester said. "We'll shoot a few seconds of grace straight on—you in the pulpit, Reverend Winters, for all of America to see," he said.

Peter Forester joined T. J. to pick up Sophie for the cemetery shoot.

"This has gone very well, T. J. I'm glad I came," he said. "I've had a good time."

"I'm glad you've had a good time," T. J. said.

"And you've not?"

"You bet I've had a great time, Peter," T. J. said.

The camera crew followed Sophie. She came out of her small cottage like a dark-eyed gloomy bride carrying a bunch of peach gladiolus and white roses, walked up the hill to Aspen and turned left to Highpoint Way where the cemetery was, built high because of the floods. From the angle of the camera focused up, the hill was powdered with light snow and white tombstones, bare slender birches and maples graceful against the horizon.

She did look lovely, T. J. thought, in her long black coat and black hair falling a little from the lavender ribbon holding a mound of curls in a loose cushion. She looked appropriately weary.

"Do you know her well?" Peter Forester asked, directing the crew to get a different angle as she entered the cemetery, walked past Mona's fresh grave—the Dickensons' plot immediately to the right—took a white rose out of the center of her own bunch of flowers and leaned over Mona's grave, putting the white rose on the bare, newly turned black earth.

"Mmm," Peter said. "Perfect shot, I think."

Then Sophie walked along a narrow, damp path to a new section of the cemetery, knelt down beside a simple high slab of marble with ANTONIO DELAURENTIS and the dates, put down her flowers and to everyone's complete surprise, certainly T. J.'s, she wept.

Pleeper Jones turned around and raised his eyebrows.

"Is she still heartbroken?" Peter asked, bemused.

"How do I know?" T. J. asked. "Maybe she adored him."

"You could have fooled me," Peter Forester said.

He looked in the camera lens. "Good. That's nice, Pleeper. We'll be able to use that at the end of one of the hours."

T. J. Wisely turned his wheelchair and started down the hill. He heard Peter Forester call him and then Sophie but he didn't turn around. He kept his head up, high up, tilted toward the sky, over the black peaked roofs of the houses, the brilliant rainbow of colors, brighter for the gray afternoon, the sprinkling of people along Main Street; he couldn't find it in his heart to look down at the perfect beauty of his beloved town.

17.

The directions to Prudential's house were simple but Helen couldn't imagine the place. A ten-minute walk, she had said. "Turn left when you leave your house, straight up the hill past the Rubins' and T. J.'s at the very top and then keep going although the road will seem to end, you'll be on a path through the woods which opens to a small clearing and a house. Not even ten minutes," she said.

The night was cool with a light wind, the sweet smell of honeysuckle in the air, a slender crescent of moon just ahead, a silver cookie low in the sky. There was very little light and, although the road was paved, Helen felt uncertain walking in such darkness.

The light was on in the Rubins' house and she could clearly see Mr. Rubin in his bedroom wandering back and forth in his pajamas, packing to go away perhaps. Mrs. Rubin opened the front door and called the cat, "Kitty kitty kitty," in a high cat-calling voice, and the cat, a fat gray one, dashed across the road in front of Helen. She didn't remember who lived in the next house—David had told her and she had forgotten but it was a modern one-story house unlike most of the houses in Meridian. There was only one light in the bedroom but through the window she could see the posts of a four-poster bed. T. J.'s house was dark inside but the yard and porch were lit by floods and she knew it was T. J.'s house although she had never been there because there was a ramp onto the front porch for a wheelchair.

After T. J.'s, it was very dark and she had difficulty seeing what actually was ahead but the paved road ended and she went into a woods which seemed less dense than ordinary woods although there was a lot of pine—a clean evergreen smell, the floor of the path crunched with sharp dry pine needles.

The scratching of pine needles reminded her of something particular. Some clear memory perhaps of Michigan in late summer. She thought of memories in white cardboard jewelry boxes, the size for a ring or a pair of earrings, obscured in the soft cotton filling—a wealth of jewels stacked in a corner of the top drawer of her mind. And it seemed now with the strong scent of Mackinaw as if one of these boxes was opening with news she wasn't certain she wanted to know.

The path went on for longer than she had expected, although halfway to the clearing the light from Prudential's house slipped through the trees, lighting the path where she was walking. Reaching the clearing, she was amazed at the tiny size of the house and its simplicity, a small wood house, two stories, one on top of the other, and lit top to bottom.

Prudential was on the porch. "Did you have trouble finding it?" she called.

"No trouble," Helen said, walking across the high grassy field, waving to her.

"So you haven't had a chance to come to my house," Prudential said, suggesting time constraints were what had made Helen's visit impossible.

"No, I haven't," Helen said.

She climbed up on the porch, high without steps, almost a jump, and Prudential grabbed her hand, leading her in the front door.

The main room was furnished in old furniture with brightly colored Indian throws and mayonnaise jars full of wildflowers on every table and walls of theater posters, a cheerful lighthearted room surprising for a woman like Prudential of no small spiritual darkness.

In the middle of the room a table was set for four with blue and white striped cloth and candles already lit.

"I don't do much entertaining," Prudential said and she seemed nervous about Helen being there. "Just last-minute like tonight when I get a chicken and it looks better than the chickens I usually get. So I call T. J. or the Winterses and, tonight, you."

The kitchen was small, with all kinds of pots and pans and pottery and pictures of vegetables and fruit on the wall and dried flowers in glasses and little jars of fresh herbs stuck in water, a cozy crowded kitchen but organized, spoons with spoons in a crockery jar, yellows with yellows, greens with greens—exactly the opposite kind of kitchen from the one Helen would have expected from Prudential, more like a kitchen in her *Country Living* magazine, with the promise of home.

The sink was full of spinach leaves soaking, a pot boiling on the stove. Prudential emptied the drain and shook the spinach.

"I love fresh spinach," she said, "cooked just so, only a minute." She smiled. "You want a beer?"

"No, thank you." Helen shook her head.

"I don't drink," Prudential said. "I used to. I'd drink and dance all night but I had to quit."

She wiped her hands on the back of her madras cotton dress.

"David's coming," she said. "At least so he said if there isn't an emergency."

She turned off some of the lights and lit the other candles in the room, lots of them, big ones. "Candles remind me of church, the smell of them does." She patted the couch. "Sit down," she said. "I'll be sitting down soon." But she didn't sit. She moved from one part of the room to the next, fussing with the table and the wildflowers in the mayonnaise jars, dusting off the back of the couch. And Helen wanted to say, "Have you gone crazy, Prudential? Who are you this evening and what is this busy charade?" But she sat on the edge of the couch, not a comfortable couch, not one made for sitting, and watched Prudential—a woman accustomed to long languid movements and slow ones—scurry around the room.

It occurred to Helen even before she heard a noise in the back room behind the kitchen that all the fussing Prudential was about had to do with making noise. That she was trying to keep Helen from hearing someone in the back room. And there was someone. Helen heard a door open just behind her.

Prudential was in the kitchen, taking the roast chicken out of the oven, mashing potatoes, but when the door opened, she stepped out of the kitchen into the main room.

"Why, hello, sweetheart," she said. "That was a very long nap."

The child was maybe three, small with a circle of black curls around a china-white face, a delicate, beautiful face, the child from "The Story of Meridian," the child Molly.

Helen caught her breath.

"You come on in now," Prudential said. "And say hello to Dr. Fielding, the new doctor I've been telling you about."

Prudential went back into the kitchen then as if nothing out of the ordinary was going on, picked up her bowl of potatoes, mashing them with her strong slender arms.

The child was in a thin nightgown, white with tiny yellow flowers, and her face was wrinkled with sleep. She folded her arms across her chest and didn't move.

"Hello," Helen said, smiling.

Molly's eyes grew round and she fixed on Helen.

"You must be Molly," Helen said.

"How did you know her name out of the blue like that?" Prudential asked.

Helen gave Prudential a look. "From the film," she said.

"I'd forgotten you've seen the film," Prudential said disingenuously.

"Enough of it to recognize Molly," Helen said.

Molly slid around the wall without turning her back on Helen, slipping into the kitchen with Prudential.

"Where's Mama?" she asked.

"Visiting," Prudential said. "Still visiting." She looked at Helen.

"We had her l-e-a-v-e," Prudential said, spelling the words so Molly couldn't understand them. "When you came to town, we said o-u-t until the visiting physician goes home."

"How come?" Helen asked.

Prudential shrugged. "You tell one lie and, before you know it, all you tell is lies."

Headlights ran over the wall before Helen had a chance to think, to accommodate to the situation, to know what to say. Prudential picked up Molly and went to the door.

"Here comes David, sweetheart."

"T. J. too?" Molly asked.

"Just David, darling," Prudential said. "T. J.'s working."

David was as cheerful as Prudential—striding into the house, kissing Molly and Prudential, kissing Helen, acting as if dining in this company was a familiar occurrence. He sat down next to Helen and took Molly on his lap, playing "Here's the church and here's the steeple," with her. And not for a minute did he betray a sense of oddness in the situation, as if the terms for this scene at Prudential's secret house were set.

They sat around the table eating chicken and mashed potatoes and spinach and hot rolls and strawberry shortcake with piles of whipped cream. The conversation was warm and pedestrian—what's up on the police blotter and who's sick and how's the garden doing, the strawberries must be from out back.

Helen began to think that she was making too much of things, that in fact Prudential had just gotten around to asking her to dinner, trusting her enough to let her in her house and she oughtn't worry about Molly. She was even having a good and easygoing time when Prudential turned to her and said in her old familiar sharp voice and attitude, "You're not a stranger to Meridian, are you?"

Helen drew her legs up under her chin, buried her face in her knees.

"Sam Durham knew you," David said, and he was gentle about it, not confrontational but clear. "When Sallie was ill and you spent the day there, you had a conversation with Sam about your

Aunt Martha and then he remembered you. We looked it up."

"Looked what up?" Helen asked.

"We remembered the name Fielding from somewhere. In a town as small as Meridian, people remember when a child dies," David said.

Helen was suddenly lightheaded. She cupped her hands, breathing the same air in and out to keep from hyperventilating.

"The name Emma Fielding means something to us," he said. "She was your sister, wasn't she?"

"I didn't mean to keep it a secret," Helen said, getting up, moving around the room, folding her arms across her chest.

Later Helen couldn't remember what happened next. T. J. arrived and Molly sat on his lap, pulling off his eye patch, hiding behind her hands. Prudential did the dishes, singing church music with the radio in the kitchen, and she and David talked about nothing in particular, sickness in Meridian, a little about Madeleine Sailor's drinking. Prudential took Molly to bed, made coffee, blew out the candles and finally they were all four of them sitting in the living room, almost silent, in the light spring air.

"So you know who I am," Helen said. She was sitting in a high-backed wooden chair, uncomfortable. She folded her legs under her. "Now you tell me what's going on in Meridian."

David did most of the talking. He sat in the hardwood chair across from Prudential, who was humming along with the conversation as if her role was musical accompaniment.

"Prudential wanted you to know about Molly," David said. "She insisted you come here tonight. She's been insisting all the time."

"It's a crazy place that keeps a child hidden from a doctor in a town," Prudential said.

"As soon as we found out you had been here when you were a little girl, that Emma Fielding, whom we all had heard about, was your sister . . . somehow it seemed out of control." T. J. shook his head. "It was as though you'd been sent here to find us out."

"Find out what?" Helen asked. "What is it that's happening?"

"What happened," Prudential said, folding her arms across her chest, throwing her great head back, "is suspicion—that's what you've been seeing with the hateful way people act to one another, creeping around, looking at their neighbors through eye slits like anybody could be carrying an automatic weapon. Tell the doctor what happened, David."

"It's not as simple as I'm going to say it," he said. And he told her about T. J. and the decision to choose Meridian for the film about an American small town. "It's probably not at all simple," he said, and he told her about Sophie and Peter Forester and about Dr. Hazelton. He was generous about Dr. Hazelton.

"We were cruel to him when he was young,"

David said. "I was cruel. He was thin and girlish and awkward and we treated him terribly."

He told her about Molly and Dr. Hazelton.

"I think he lost his head when he was taking care of Molly that morning."

"But why did you hide her?" Helen asked.

"We hid her until the film crew left so they wouldn't know our secret. We didn't want them to know that we were anything less than the town they had invented for the television film. And then when we had to have a doctor because of the children getting sick, we hid her from you," he said. "A doctor gets to know everything about a small town and we didn't want you to know about Molly."

They stayed up late talking and talking. Finally Prudential went to bed and T. J. said he had to go home or he'd die of exhaustion.

It was dawn when David took T. J. to his house and then drove Helen. She was almost asleep on her feet as he walked her up to the door. She leaned against him with her body weight, hard against him as if this evening he were large enough to carry her weight and his own.

"Whew," she said, lifting his large hand, kissing his fingers.

18.

Helen was hallucinating children.

It is a soft measured sunny day—a spread of lawn, maybe the back garden of her childhood home in Ann Arbor. The lawn checkered with sprinklers watering the grass with children, tiny children popping out of the holes in the sprinkler, ballooning upward and upward, flying children spilling on the long green lawn, rolling over and over as they hit the earth. The garden is filling with children and Helen cannot breathe.

She woke up in bed in Dr. Hazelton's house, lying flat without a pillow, the room spinning as if she were drunk, and she grabbed the side, pulling herself to a sitting position, turning on the light.

It was 4 A.M., she thought, and she was unraveling again. She could see her mind like a tight ball of twine, undoing itself, slipping across the hardwood floor.

She made a mental list of the last few hours. She'd been at Prudential's for dinner and there was the child Molly and David and T. J. and she drank too much wine.

She had said she was too tired to walk home

and David had driven her in the patrol car, stopping first to let T. J. out at his house.

The next thing Helen remembered, he was leaning down over her face and she was sleeping.

"You're at home," he'd said.

Home, home, home, home, came through her sleep.

"Come home, Helen, hurry, Helen," her mother is saying. "I'm here on the front porch waiting for you."

And swinging across her vision is a faded color photograph of her mother on the front porch of their house in Ann Arbor before Emma died—her lovely mother, just out of girlhood, in a yellow dress, her hair long and breezy, a small sunflower stuck behind her ear.

She got out of bed, showered and dressed for the day although morning would not begin for several hours. But anxious to erase the images of raining children crowding her brain, she went downstairs, turned on the television and put in the third cassette of "The Story of Meridian," fast-forwarding to Dr. Richard Hazelton. It was easy to find him even with the images flashing across the screen—he was a white, white figure dancing by and she stopped the moving picture and examined it as if under a microscope, looking at each detail of his face—Dr. Hazelton on the front steps of the clinic, Dr. Hazelton with Molly on his lap, the back of him, and Dr. Hazelton recognizable from the long, long arms, standing in line at the pharmacy, bending to speak to a small young curly-haired woman with a lollipop.

Summer in the shade under a leafy tree, Helen sits on the ground with a stick making pictures in the dirt in the triangle made by her outstretched legs. She can see her parents from where she is sitting and they're laughing like bells.

Emma is standing beside her mother, pulling on her long lavender skirt, a striped skirt, lavender and white stripes and shiny. Helen sees her but she keeps her head down, pretending to look at the Bengal tiger she has drawn in the dirt on the ground in front of her.

"Helen," her mother calls, looking over at the tree where Helen is sitting. But she keeps her head down and doesn't answer. "Helen?"

"Helen," her father calls. "Helen."

Her mother is barefooted, pretty bare feet with red polish on the toes, a lavender and white striped skirt, just above the ankles, but Helen doesn't look up.

"Darling," her mother says, "I'd love it if you'd take Emma for a little walk just now so your father and I can finish our supper.

"Helen?"

She looks up. Her mother is holding Emma in her arms, Emma's plump arms wrapped tight around her neck.

"No," Helen says.

"Helen." Her father's voice drops like a rock on her small head. "Take Emma for a walk down the wildflower path to the river. Bring us back some flowers."

"By the time you get back, we'll be finished supper and we can do something lovely with you," her mother says. "Here." Her mother puts Emma down beside her. "You take Emma's hand and I'll take Daddy's."

They are walking back to the picnic table, hand in hand, her father bending toward her mother, bending over her, kissing her hair. "Be careful of Emma," he calls.

"Be careful of Emma," her mother calls but they don't turn around or wave or smile or notice that Helen has gone down the wildflower path to her destiny.

On television, there is a story of two little girls, familiar girls to Helen, she has seen their pictures. The older, the larger, a tall dark-haired whimsy of a girl, is holding the hand of the younger, plumper, sweet-faced, yellow-haired girl. The camera focuses on the hands laced together. The older girl lifts the hands of both, turning them so the soft plump baby hand is on top. And then the camera moves up the body of the dark-haired older girl, close up so she fills the screen in pieces, to her face on which there is a look of—is hatred too strong a word? The angle changes and what Helen sees in the soundless landscape is a closeup of both children, the older one looking down without affection at the plump baby hand on top of her own.

Helen dials her mother in New York. It is so late at night or so early in the morning that there is a chance her mother will by accident answer the phone and then she can capture her, hold on to her voice at the other end.

It rings again and again and then, in her mother's small musical voice, out of sleep, "Hello."

"Mama," Helen says and she is a child again, pure child, no distance on her broken heart and no defense. "I am going crazy. You have to help me."

There's a hesitation. A brief hesitation, a split second to throw a net over her mother's head and drag her in. "Please talk to me."

Maybe you will have no daughters, Mother, Helen thinks but she doesn't say anything. Maybe I will die of grief unless you can help me now. She is silent, waiting, waiting.

"I'm going to change phones," her mother says.

There is a pause, a long silence and then a click.

"I know you've called because you want to know what happened on the day that Emma died," Allie Fielding said and her voice was stronger, more certain than Helen had heard it for years.

"I would be grateful," Helen said, her heart

beating so fast, she thought she would die of it before she heard what her mother was going to tell her and she knew that this time she was going to find out.

From the other end of a tunnel, a long sewer pipe to eternity, her mother's voice. "I don't know what happened that day," she said. "It was a lovely, warm evening, my anniversary, and I bought champagne and wanted to be alone with your father. I wanted for you and Emma to go off and play." Her voice was soft and clear. "I don't remember what went on at all because I was drunk." From a great distance, but distinctly, clearly, "What happened to Emma was my fault."

19.

The telephone was ringing and ringing. Helen heard it somewhere in the back of her brain but she was sleeping too soundly to separate the ringing from sleep. When she woke up she was sitting in a chair in front of the television, the television blank, the last cassette of "The Story of Meridian" playing while she was sleeping in front of it. It was daylight, after 6 A.M. She picked up the telephone. There was no voice on the other end. She knew in her sensible brain that no one was there, although in her ear the voice she heard was Richie Hazelton's, Dr. Richard Hazelton's voice before it had changed to the voice of a man.

"Hello, Helen Fielding?" he said.

Helen is standing on the bank of the river Meryn, her arms folded, Emma in the dirt making pictures with a stick. Kneeling beside her is a young boy about ten—Helen remembers—not a boy she likes particularly, rather a strange boy and one who worries her with his long, long arms and white skin and way of staring at Helen as if he wished to harm her.

He has come out of the bushes beside the bank, out of nowhere.

"I was fishing," he says. "What are you doing by the river?"

"Mama made me walk Emma to the river," Helen says.

He takes Emma's plump hand. "Hi, Emma," he says.

Emma looks up without speaking. Perhaps she isn't talking yet.

"Wanna go swimming?" he asks her.

"She can't swim," Helen says. "I can't swim either. I can't put my head under."

"I'm just going to have her wade," he says, picking Emma up. "Just pretend swimming."

Helen watches him walk down to the river, Emma cooing happily, gripping the back of his shirt with her small fist. He holds her over the water, letting it lap and tickle her bare feet. She is squealing with excitement and delight.

"Be careful of Emma," she says over her sister's happy cries.

"I'll be careful," he calls.

She doesn't see the next moment, blinking or looking over Richie Hazelton's head or to the side, only a split second, the speed of light, of sound, no time to change the course of their lives.

And Emma is swimming downriver, her yellow sundress a bright moon in the middle of the gray-black hurrying water.

"She's swimming," Richie Hazelton says and his voice has the cry of hysteria.

"No," Helen screams. "She can't swim. Please get her. Please catch her."

"I can't catch her," he calls, running down the path in the direction that Emma is tumbling and tumbling downriver, away from them. Helen cannot run after her. Standing on the path with her hands over her eyes, she cannot breathe.

Years later, it seems years later, a lifetime, Helen, still standing on the bank with her eyes covered, hears Richie Hazelton coming toward her through the leaves littered on the path.

"She's gone," he says flatly.

And he kneels down beside her at eye level, looks at her directly with his cold blue eyes.

"If you tell," he says coolly, "I'll kill you."

Helen was screaming. She couldn't help herself. A sound roared out of her belly that she had never heard before, shattering the morning. It came and came and she stood in the living room of Dr. Hazelton's house, unable to change directions, an odd witness to her own unstoppable grief.

She picked up the telephone and called David Jaspersen.

"I believe Dr. Hazelton has Maggie Sailor," Helen said.

"Dr. Hazelton?" David said.

"I have a feeling he's at the river with her, maybe even right now."

"What makes you think that?" he asked.

"I have a reason to think it," Helen said, and even now in her mind she could see him on the riverbank with Maggie and he was going to put her in the water to see if she could swim.

There was a moment of silence.

"All right," David said quietly. "We'll go check. I'll call Prudential. If you're right, we should bring Prudential."

The night before, after her call to her mother, Helen had fallen asleep almost immediately, drugged by the conversation. It was her instinct to sit still as if she were too fragile, actually fragile, with breakable arms and legs. So she waited for sleep. She had no dreams but rather a sense of weightlessness, in a tiny corner of the earth from which gravity had slipped and, though the absence of weight was joy in its pure freedom, it was too close to death for pleasure. She felt as if she were tumbling into an open space with nothing to hold her feet on the ground.

In the patrol car she sat next to Prudential, pressing against her as if the back seat of the car was too small for both of them. Prudential's flesh was compensatory and gave Helen a feeling she longed to have of confinement, holding her down, keeping her insides from escaping the thin protection of her own skin.

Prudential lifted her head up, looking out the window away from Helen.

"I apologize for lying," she said matter-of-factly.

"You didn't actually lie," Helen said. "You just didn't tell the truth."

"I lied," Prudential said. "You asked me the first day you were here did I know a Molly and I said no when Molly was living in my house. I apologize for that."

They drove on in silence. The sun was rising as they drove east, blinding through the windshield, and Helen closed her eyes.

"We'll park just at the entrance," said T. J., who sat with David in the front seat.

"It's a big park," David said. "I'll let you out and drive along the road periphery to the park and, T. J., you can go through the open fields since I don't think the wheelchair will go down the path to the river."

"I'll go down the path to the river," Helen said.

"You know that path?" David asked. "It's been there since I can remember."

"We weren't allowed to go down alone because someone died there once. Do you remember that, David?"

"I remember," David said.

"We didn't know who died," T. J. said. "Someone. Parents said someone. I used to ask and nobody seemed to know."

"It was probably my sister," Helen said.

It was just before seven when they left the car, the air clear and lovely, the sun flooding the horizon with a bright silky light, shimmering over the purple field, the path to the river cheerful with the sounds of insects chattering, the cries of birds.

The two women walked along briskly, Prudential taller but walking slightly perpendicular to the ground, dragging her foot, so their heads from a distance were even, just skirting the tops of the unmowed grasses sprinkled with color.

"We made a mistake," Prudential said.

"You mean about Molly?"

"I mean about lying," Prudential said to settle the score, heading down the path to Judgment Day. "I don't believe in sin but if I did, what we did was sinful."

"Who is we?" Helen asked.

"The town," Prudential said. "We got taken away with the picture of things and didn't want bad news in the film."

"You don't seem like the type," Helen said. "I'm sure it wasn't your fault."

"I didn't do anything to stop it." She picked a long reed and stuck it in her mouth, pulling it through her teeth. "Do you believe in God?" she asked.

"No," Helen said. "But I believe. I'm afraid if I didn't believe, I'd be struck dead." She laughed. "So if I'm afraid, then I must believe," she said. "Do you?"

"Uh-huh," Prudential said. "I don't believe in God."

Helen let her hand swing to touch Prudential's.

"Scared?" Prudential asked.

"A little," Helen said.

"I don't think we're going to find anything except the river," Prudential said.

"But listen," Helen said.

They stopped.

"Can you hear it?" Helen asked. "The water was high when I was here earlier and now you can hear it rushing over the rocks."

"I don't like water," Prudential said. "I like the earth and not the air and not the sea." She folded her arms across her chest. "Maggie's not at the river," she said sourly. "I doubt she's still alive."

"You really think not?" Helen asked.

"That's what I think."

They were coming to the clearing. Helen could tell by the sudden suffusion of light.

"Shh," Prudential said, taking hold of Helen's arm. They stopped and stood very still.

Helen listened. She heard the insect life and birds and was it voices, she wondered, holding her breath to listen above the sound of her own breathing.

"Quietly," Prudential said, moving ahead just a little, and they crept slowly along through the thick grasses swishing by them as they went.

It was strange, Helen thought later, how you know the unseen even though it's invisible, as if the presence of everything desired is in the mind as a suggestion, a whisper of truth.

She knew before the path opened like stage curtains onto the banks of the river Meryn that a child would be on the riverbank. She felt her presence and, lightheaded, too faint to catch her breath, she took hold of Prudential.

What Helen saw was Emma Fielding on the ground beside the river, her legs stretched out, making a triangle of dirt on which she was drawing with a stick. She was larger than Helen remembered, maybe five, Helen's age at the time she had disappeared, and she was wearing a sunny yellow dress, her hair tied up in a ribbon.

Leaning against a tree just behind her, watching her draw in the dirt, was a tall pale-skinned man with long arms.

"Dr. Hazelton," Prudential said.

He turned, his hands in his pockets, in no hurry. He ran his fingers through his hair.

"Hello, Prudential," he said.

The child looked up toward the field where Helen and Prudential were standing but she didn't move or show any recognition of Prudential at all. She simply sat with her legs out and looked at them curiously.

"Maggie?" Prudential said in a soft velvet voice.

The child tilted her head.

"Your mama's been looking for you."

Helen took a step toward him and they were looking at each other directly across the space of land.

"Dr. Hazelton?"

He crossed his arms tight over his chest.

"I'm Helen Fielding," she said. "Do you remember me?"

She couldn't tell from his face whether he remembered her. His expressions moved through surfaces like developing photographs.

"I'm a doctor here now," Helen said. "Since this legionella epidemic. Since you left."

"I see," he said. His face looked shattered, reflected in a mirror of broken glass. He put his hand up to cover his mouth as if he were about to scream.

"Are you Emma Fielding's sister?" he asked. "I remember Emma."

"Do you remember what happened to her?"

He nodded. "Of course. I remember," he said. "I let her go."

A brilliant yellow sun moved over the horizon,

drawing a shaft of light between them, too bright for Helen to see Richard Hazelton's face washed bone white in the sunlight. But she could see him sinking to the ground, folding in on himself as if he were made of strips of cardboard. And she heard him across the distance before she turned to follow Maggie and Prudential down the path to the park.

"It was an accident, Dr. Fielding," he said. "I didn't mean to harm her."

20.

Dr. Hazelton was dead.

He was discovered by a member of the Harrisville police force in a thicket beside the river. An autopsy conducted in Harrisville revealed that he had died of an overdose of a combination of drugs taken shortly after Helen and Prudential walked with Maggie down the path back to the park. He must have concealed himself in dense brush, taken the drugs and lain down, for he was found lying on his side with his knees up and his arms twisted as if at the last moment and in spite of his intentions he had thrashed for air.

⋆ ⋆ ⋆

Maggie Sailor said that Dr. Hazelton had been kind to her, reading her stories, buying her ice cream, taking her to the movies.

"He wouldn't let me come home and I was homesick," she said. "But he wasn't ever mean. He said I'd get to go home someday, not long from now, and that nothing bad would happen to me with him."

Sometime in the spring Dr. Hazelton had bought a truck because on the day of Maggie's disappearance he had come with a truck to Meridian. Maggie said she was standing outside the drugstore waiting for her mother when he leaned out the window and said, "Hi, Maggie," and she was glad to see him and climbed into the driver's seat with him when he asked her if she'd like to see the instruments on his new truck. That was all she remembered. He did something to her that made her go to sleep. But he didn't hurt her.

In Meridian, in spite of what had happened, Dr. Hazelton was mourned.

The church hall at First Methodist filled up, people arriving with food: fruit pies and chocolate cakes and potato casseroles and noodles, chicken and sausage, macaroni and cheese, bottles of Gallo wine and beer. After the news of Dr. Hazelton's death had traveled through town, they gathered in the church hall. By that afternoon the church hall was full, as if the flood dikes of suspicion dominating the spirit of Meridian since the film crew left had given way, spilling the population down the hills to the large cup at the bottom of town where First Methodist was located.

"I don't understand it," Helen said to Prudential after Maggie was found. "He kidnapped a child. And what about Molly?"

"Things aren't so simple," Prudential said. "I suppose we feel to blame for what happened to him, how he got in such a state of mind to do what he did."

"If you say so," Helen said, sitting in a swivel chair in the waiting room across from Prudential, eating a chicken sandwich.

"It's hard to know very much about a person or a place," Prudential said, braiding her long hair. "There's going to be a funeral tomorrow afternoon."

"David told me," Helen said.

"My guess is that the whole town will turn out," Prudential said solemnly. "Even the Sailors."

Helen was bone weary but well—better than she had been for many weeks, maybe for years. She felt a kind of internal settlement as if the myriad cardboard shapes that filled in the jigsaw face of Helen Fielding—the one that Oliver used to keep on the dining table, half finished—were in place. She was lightheaded, lifted off the ground.

She had written to her parents, sending the same letter to both of them.

Dear Mama and Daddy,

I don't know if what I imagined happening when Emma disappeared is what actually happened but this is what I saw in my mind's eye on the bank of the river the evening of your anniversary, June 28, twenty-five years ago.

And she told the story of Dr. Hazelton.

At the end of the letter she wrote:

I'm not sure why I couldn't remember Richie Hazelton was there. I suppose I was so afraid he would kill me as he promised he would do if I did tell that I forgot until I came back to Meridian and all the memories flooded in.

P.S. Thank you for telling me about the circumstances of your anniversary, Mama. That news has made all of the difference in my life.

I'll be going home soon. Maybe this week. The epidemic is over in Meridian and they no longer need a visiting physician.

"I'm going back to South Carolina soon," Prudential said, sensing a wind change, brushing the crumbs off her lap.

"You can't," Helen said.

"I beg your pardon." Prudential got up, stacked the files of the morning's patients and started to put them away.

"They need you here," Helen said.

"They've got you."

"No," Helen said, leaning against the desk,

her arms folded. "I'm the one who should go home. I've done what I came here to do."

Prudential shrugged. "Well, don't worry about me," she said combatively. "I was fine before you came so it won't break me in two for you to leave."

She got out the files for the afternoon clinic patients. "So will you go to Dr. Hazelton's funeral?"

"What time is it?"

"One-thirty tomorrow," Prudential said, opening the folders, making the list of afternoon patients.

"I'll be there," Helen said.

She had not told Prudential she was leaving tomorrow, going home, back to Ann Arbor on the three forty-eight to Detroit. She would tell her maybe later, but no one else. She wanted to slip away quietly, no gestures of appreciation from the town, no ceremonies, just a quick sail through town like weather as if she'd never been or was returning in another form or would come back later, predictable as rain.

David Jaspersen was sitting on her front porch reading the Harrisville paper when Helen came home from the clinic.

She kissed him on the lips. She had wanted to, planned to kiss him all the way down the block and up the steps, knowing that the gesture would be an announcement. She saw him from a distance sitting on the top step of her porch with the newspaper and she was moved to see him there, feeling a kinship as if there were something similar between her and this man David Jaspersen, the chief of police—who had made an error in judgment, a wrong decision, and hurt people who mattered to him. And though, of course, there was nothing similar and she had been a child when Emma died, making no decision except perhaps the wish in the darkest of her dreams not to be careful of Emma, she felt close to him, struck by the ambiguity of the film's heroic policeman and the young troubled man on her front steps who would not resign from his job although he had failed at it. In a peculiar way, he seemed to her blighted and salvageable—heroic in his humanness.

"I bought dinner," he said. "T. J. may come later. He's at the Sailors' talking to Maggie." He followed her into the house. "Fresh salmon," he said, taking the pink fish out of the grocery bag. "We never get fresh salmon in Ohio."

Helen peered into the bag.

"Champagne?"

"It's a celebration."

"Of what?" Helen asked.

"Of the miracle doctor."

She laughed. "That's lovely, David, even though it isn't true."

They cooked together, Helen washing asparagus, scrubbing potatoes, chopping dill, David cleaning the salmon, opening champagne.

She took off her shoes, slipped into a chair, lifting her glass of champagne to him.

"Who will live here when I leave?" Helen asked.

"You're not leaving," he said.

"In case I leave," she said.

"Probably Prudential. She'll be the doctor here if you go and this is the doctor's house." He put the salmon under the broiler and sat down next to her, taking her hand, inspecting it, turning it over in his as though he had not examined a hand before.

"I want to know one other thing," Helen said. "Did you paint my wall?"

David laughed. "Me?" He shook his head. "I'm too chicken for that."

"So who did it?"

"Madeleine," David said.

"Madeleine?" Helen asked. "Did you know all the time?"

"I found out today," David said. "She's written you a letter of apology and called to read it to me."

Helen put her head down in her folded arms.

David touched her hair. "You must be exhausted," he said.

"A little, I suppose," she replied.

There was something she wanted to say to him, not yet formed in her mind, which had to do with the future, with seeing him later but just wishing for that, something she had never wished for in her hello-good-bye love affairs, made her suddenly shy.

He pinched out the candles with his fingers.

"I suppose you think I'm awful because of all this," he said.

She looked over at him through the smoke.

"I wasn't there so I don't know," Helen said. "I don't understand why you didn't go after Dr. Hazelton."

"At the time it seemed crucial to protect the reputation of the town," David said. "We seemed to be in an emergency situation."

Helen shrugged.

"I guess you'll leave soon," he said. "Everything's in place here."

"I will," Helen said. "Probably soon. Prudential can handle things."

"It's too bad." He poured her another glass of wine.

"That I'm leaving?"

"Just the way things fell out."

Later, after dinner, sitting in the living room, her brain slippery from champagne, she turned on the television to the last cassette of "The Story of Meridian."

They sat on the couch, Helen leaning against David's shoulder.

"When they filmed this section, it was Friday and Molly had been found and was in the hospital," David said. "They filmed all the weekend events and then packed up and were gone by Saturday morning."

"Whatever happened with Sophie and the director?" Helen asked.

"Nothing," David said. "As far as I know, they've never been in touch. We asked Sophie to leave town when you came because Sophie's a talker and we didn't want a stranger to know what had happened here."

The last day opens with a baseball game on the high school grounds, the boys in bright red and white uniforms, playing without jackets, although it is clear even from the film that it is cold outside. The game fades to a meeting of the choir and then a frame of Ben Winters in the pulpit of First Methodist speaking on grace and the Sunday school classes with Sallie Durham talking about Easter and what happens when a person dies and what happened to Jesus when he died and did he die after all, and is dead dead or not.

"I remember my Grandmother Durham," Sallie is saying matter-of-factly. "She had blue hair and made me ginger cookies with white icing and now she's dead."

After church, after the closeups in the church hall of all of the people who had principal roles in the film, the camera slips over their heads, over the trees and up the eastern hills of Meridian, over the rooftops, sliding down to a peach frame house into the garden where Molly DeLaurentis leans against a tree, holding a stuffed animal, maybe a bear, face in against her jacket and looking off into the middle distance.

And then the camera follows her gaze down Poplar Street, over Main behind the railroad station to the river Meryn, a creek at first, growing wider and wider, filling the television so the credits as they roll down the screen appear over the whitecaps and there is no sound but that of the river headed south.

At the services for Dr. Hazelton, Helen sat next to Prudential at the back of the church. She was weepy. She couldn't help herself.

The church was full, people in the aisles, children in their parents' arms—the Durhams were there, Sallie Durham gave Helen a little wave, and Maria Walker stood with Laura O'Connor. Edie Winters walked up the aisle with the Sailors, Maggie between them, beaming and beaming—they couldn't help themselves.

"I'm surprised at all these children coming," Helen said to Prudential.

"Dying shouldn't be any more remarkable than living is what I think," Prudential said.

"And Maggie?" Helen asked. "Do you think she knows how Dr. Hazelton died?"

"No, not that," Prudential said.

T. J. came just as the opening hymn began and stopped his wheelchair next to the aisle where Helen was sitting, blowing her a kiss.

The organ rose above the congregation and everyone was singing and then David Jaspersen got up to speak. He spoke about Dr. Hazelton. Saying good things about his work in Meridian, and telling of the way he was treated sometimes with cruelty by other boys, including himself, because he was different. He talked about Meridian and Maggie and the Sailors and Molly, he thanked Helen for coming and then he talked about "The Story of Meridian."

"Before the television crew came here," he said, "we had a sense of who we were, neither more nor less than other people, and that seemed satisfactory and safe. And then we fell in love with our image on film, losing sight of what was real in our lives and what was not.

"It wasn't the fault of television or even the television's portrayal of us. It was our fault for believing it."

And then he walked down the steps to the pulpit, down the three short steps from the altar and sat down.

It was a long service, with memorials and the children's choir and Sandy Case singing "Amazing Grace" and finally Henry Sailor reading a prayer for the congregation.

Helen slipped out during the final hymn just before the recessional. She kissed Prudential's hand, touched T. J. on the face as she crossed by him and left by the side door into a brilliant cool late spring afternoon.

She looked back to see if David Jaspersen had come out but he had been at the front of the church and would be among the last to leave. She had written him a note.

Dear David, I'm going back to Ann Arbor today. I hope you'll come. Love, Helen.

She had told only Prudential that she was leaving but it seemed the right thing to do, to leave silently and quickly while Meridian, Ohio, shaken by the long passage of spring, folded inward to recover. Maybe she would return. Maybe she would be a visitor again.

She hurried up the hill from First Methodist, past Aunt Martha's, no longer Aunt Martha's. There was no Emma in her mind's eye on the front porch, no child at all, only a familiar house belonging to a stranger. She rushed past her offices at the clinic, the police station and pharmacy and library and ice cream shop, arriving at Meridian railway station glittering in the pure light of late May just as the three forty-eight to Detroit lumbered into town.

The stationmaster handed her the bags she had left with him earlier in the day. "See you later," he called. "Hurry, Dr. Fielding. Trains only stop for a minute in Meridian."

And she ran to the platform, climbing up the steps into the coach, which was empty except for a young girl in a pale rose sundress who sat in the middle of a seat, her hands folded, a wrapped lollipop in her fist.

Helen looked around and sat down on the seat beside her.

"Mind?" she asked.

The young girl shook her head. "I'm glad," she said. "I've been alone since Louisville."

The train moved slowly out of town past the town's sign WELCOME TO MERIDIAN, the CBS advertisement for "The Story of Meridian," half hidden by the poster of a missing child. At the end of Main Street it picked up speed, hurtling past the fields outside of town and along the river as it widened and widened through the dusky gray windows beside Helen, filling her view.

IF YOU HAVE ENJOYED READING THIS LARGE PRINT BOOK AND YOU WOULD LIKE MORE INFORMATION ON HOW TO ORDER A WHEELER LARGE PRINT BOOK, PLEASE WRITE TO: